Incident
on the Way to
a Killing

MICHAEL HAMMONDS

DOUBLEDAY & COMPANY, INC.
GARDEN CITY, NEW YORK
1977

All of the characters in this book
are fictitious, and any resemblance
to actual persons, living or dead,
is purely coincidental.

Library of Congress Cataloging in Publication Data

Hammonds, Michael.
Incident on the way to a killing.

I. Title.
PZ4.H2265In [PS3558.A454]   813'.5'4
ISBN: 0-385-12569-0
Library of Congress Catalog Card Number 76-42332

For Bill Priestley,
companyero

*Incident
on the Way to
a Killing*

CHAPTER 1

They came in the dark of the morning. The rattle of horses' hooves echoed in the cold June morning as the riders came through the back gate of Calder's Post.

Standing at the bar of the main store, eating a breakfast of pancakes, potatoes, and venison, Lake Mattick's eyes jerked up at the sound. His hand started for the Henry rifle on the bar next to him, then, frowning, he remembered where he was.

"War's over," the bartender said from the far end of the bar.

Lake peered at him. A shadow in the coal-oil light, the bartender was tending at the wood cookstove behind the planking that had been put up as a bar. His face was blurred by the light, and that bothered Lake a little. He couldn't remember what he looked like.

"That's what I hear," Mattick replied and, turning, walked to the window.

The riders passed the store and angled toward the barns. Four men. Shadows dressed in fur and leather, carrying Hawken rifles in the crooks of their arms and leading three other horses. Lake's eyes followed the men. The heavy fur coats warped them slightly, making them seem like bears on horseback.

Too accustomed to uniforms, he thought, glancing down at his own clothing. Most of it was left from his uniform. Caped cavalry greatcoat, blue jumper and trousers, and on his head a "Jeff Davis" Kossuth hat that had seen better days. On the bar was the Henry and leaning against his bedroll, under the slab wood, was a Chicopee saber. Echoes. Visible fragments of another time. Blinking, he turned back to the bar.

"That them?" he asked the bartender.

"Yeah, Rufe and the boys. They're headin' down to the barn for the pack frames and supplies."

Lake could see his face now. Grinning and curious. And still a shadow in the half-light.

"Lot of fellas just to be escortin' one woman."

"Seein's how her husband owns this whole kit and caboodle, probably ain't enough. Hell, the way she is—"

Lake picked up his fork. "You know her?"

"Well, no," the bartender sniffed. "Heard about her though—"

"Yeah." Lake nodded, cutting him off, and stabbed at the pancakes.

The bartender eyed him for a moment. "This fella you were askin' about? Quincy?"

Lake's throat tightened and, frowning, he put the forkful of pancakes down.

"What about him?"

"Nothin'." The bartender shook his head. "Just you called him Major. You in the war together? Friends?"

"We were in the war together," Lake answered tersely.

"Just kinda funny." The bartender shrugged. "Don't meet anybody from that war at all, then all of a sudden two of you. And bein' friends and all. Never got to talk to anybody 'at was really in it. Was gonna join myself, but—"

"Yeah." Lake nodded. "How much?"

"For the food?"

"Yeah."

"Fifteen cents, but you—"

Lake fished the coins from his pants pocket and put them on the bar. "Thanks." He nodded and, reaching down, he picked up the saber and his bedroll.

"Where you headed?" the bartender asked.

"The barn."

"You got time yet. Wanted to ask you—"

"I'm in a hurry," Lake said.

The bartender shrugged, watching him. "Old Rufe'll get you to Cunningham's," he said. "That is unless Mrs.

Calder changes her mind like Rufe says she ought to." The bartender looked down at Lake's plate. "Hey, mister, you didn't even finish."

———◆———

Across the stockade, Maggie Calder held the curtain away from the oilpaper window and watched the riders cross toward the barn.

The two men in the lead, she knew. Rufus Kitrel and Dick Summers. Once mountain men, now scouts for her husband's freight company. The other two, she only knew by sight and name. A thin, red-haired youth named Tim Carmody and a short stocky man, Euripides Hanks, who the men had naturally christened Shorty. Euripides, or Shorty, he hadn't had much luck with names. "You set old Shorty's proper name on end," Rufe Kitrel had once said to her, "why it'd be taller than he is."

The riders hesitated, then Shorty and Tim Carmody turned toward her, and Rufe and Dick Summers continued down toward the barns.

Her stomach trembled, as the two men approached the house. It was time.

Releasing the curtain, she was turning back into the room when the movement of another figure pulled her gaze back. Coming out of the door of the store.

It was a man. Hurrying. Nearly running. A hat pulled down over his eyes, a blue greatcoat curling back in the wind. He came down the steps and angled toward the barn.

Turning back into the room, Maggie walked to the bed where her carpetbag lay open. She checked through it, ruffling dresses and petticoats with her hands, then walked to the full-length mirror across the room.

In the dark light, the shadowed glass outlined a tall woman in her mid-twenties. Wide-shouldered and high-breasted. Dressed in a linen shirt, brown corduroy jacket, and tan nankeen pants pushed into high-heeled Napoleon leg boots. On the dresser next to the mirror were a black slouch hat and a brown chesterfield coat. The coat was too expensive to be worn horseback riding perhaps, but it was warm, and in this country that was what mattered.

Buttoning the jacket, she stepped toward the clothes on the dresser. A knock on the door stopped her. Frowning, she looked at it. The knock came again. A little harder this time.

"Come in," she answered, and crossed to the dresser.

The door pushed open and Maggie half-turned to see Mary Warren's short stocky figure come into the room.

"They're here," Mary said.

"I know." Maggie nodded. Slipping into the chester-field and fitting the hat on her head, she turned to Mary.

There was a slight gloss of wetness in Mary's eyes and a line of disapproval tautening her mouth.

"You . . . look like a man," Mary said.

"I mean to be warm. Riding in a dress would be foolish."

Mary nodded stiffly. "Perhaps, but there is a proper way of doing things." She started to turn, and Maggie reached out, touching her arm, stopping her.

"I'm sorry, Mary," she said. "I don't want us to part with bad feelings."

Mary Warren turned back into the room, and Maggie

glanced up and around. "Funny how decisions finally become . . . final, isn't it?"

"It's what you wanted."

"Yes"—Maggie nodded—"but that doesn't make it any easier."

"It's not easy for John either."

Maggie's eyes came around. "I know that. I'm not doing this to hurt him."

The hardness lined Mary Warren's mouth again. "That really doesn't help him, you know, or make it any different. I've been your friend for five years, Maggie, and I think what you're doing is disgraceful. What will you do?"

"I don't know," Maggie answered. "I haven't thought that far ahead yet. Work in a store perhaps."

"If anyone will have you. You can still change your mind—"

"No," she replied quickly, and her voice softened. "I can't do that," she whispered and, walking to her bed, she closed her bag, pulling the straps tightly around it and buckling them; she picked it up and walked by Mary into the next room. In the door, she saw the gawky form of Tim Carmody waiting.

"Mrs. Calder." His right hand touched the front of his hat. "Rufe and Dick are down to the barn gettin' frames. You can wait here till they—"

"No," Maggie cut in. "I'll go with you now," she said and turned back to Mary Warren.

They stood like strangers looking at each other, the five years they'd known each other gone. Whispered away in one moment of decision. Like the changing of masks.

"Thank you," Maggie finally managed, not knowing what else to say. "Take care. . . ."

"You too. . . ."

Nodding, Maggie touched her friend on the arm, then hurried out the door.

Rufe Kitrel and Dick Summers rode into the barn and dismounted. Patting his blue roan aside, Rufe stretched, then rubbed his graying beard. "I'll get the packs if—"

"I'll do it," Dick said. "You water the saddle horses."

Rufe looked at his friend of twenty years. A hint of a smile pushed at his lips. "Givin' me the easy end of it."

"Rather do it myself," Dick nodded, going into the stall where the pack frames were hung. Reaching up he pulled two down. "Ever' time you pack the horses, I have a helluva time findin' things."

Rufe's smile pushed wider. "You know besides gettin' bald in your old age, you're gettin' crabby too."

"Just that your mind ain't on it," Dick said, bringing the pack frames out and looking them over. "Never is. Longer we stay at this, the more you get like a moonin' kid."

Rufe frowned and scratched his graying beard. "True enough, I reckon," he allowed, then shook his head. "Now they got us playin' nursemaid . . ." he grumbled.

"What?"

"Said they got us playin' nursemaid."

"Thought you liked her."

"I do." Rufe nodded, then added, "In a way. Hell, for two cents—"

"You ain't got the two cents," Dick reminded him. "That's why we're playin' nursemaid."

"Yeah," Rufe sighed and began gathering up the reins to the saddle horses.

"Look on the bright side," Dick said, as Rufe started down the aisle of the barn.

"What's that?"

"Least we'll get to see old Cotton Adams."

Rufe looked back at Dick. "He still bartendin' at Cunningham's?"

"Last I heard."

Rufe grinned. "Remember him at that rendezvous at the Hole. Swear he nearly rode that grizzly."

"Couple of more jugs and he would have."

"Yeah," Rufe sighed, and the smile faded. "Yeah," he said quietly and, turning, he led the horses down the aisle of the barn and out the door into the corral. A stream ran through the far corner, and Rufe led the horses down and let them push their muzzles into the cold running water.

As the horses drank, Rufe stood looking out across the fences to the barren brown hills and the Leyenda Mountains beyond. Heavy clouds moved across them, shrouding them, making them seem farther away than they were.

"Where I oughta be," the old man sighed, then heard someone come into the corral behind him.

Glancing back, he watched a blue-uniformed man come down from the barn leading a big Morgan gelding.

"Didn't know the Army'd moved in." The old man nodded.

"They haven't," the young man smiled. "Just one mustered-out lieutenant." He nodded toward the mountains. "Looks like rain."

"Maybe." Rufe nodded. "Most likely snow."

The young man looked up. "Snow? In June?"

Rufe smiled patiently. "In June," he said, nodding. "Worse snow I ever seen come in June. Some places back up there, it snows year round."

The uniformed man's eyes narrowed skeptically. "Not that I doubt your word, just that it's a little hard to believe."

Rufe sniffed distastefully. "Lot of things hard to believe about this country. 'Specially to Easterners. Ever'thin's got to be in order for'em. Straight lines and logic. This country ain't straight lines and logic. Nothin' on that goddamn prairie but a lot of lonesome and hard times. Seen folks try to settle it, but they never make it. Hell, there's some Bible-beaters near the mountains tryin' it a couple of years ago, but I don't see how they'll make it."

"Bible-beaters?"

"Religious folks that don't like any other religious folks. Started'em a town out there. Called it New Eden, I think." He smiled sourly. "Helluva name for anything out there. Prairie'll kill a man in the blink of an eye. Nothin' to landmark on. Easiest country I ever seen to get lost in."

The young man smiled wanly. "I found that out."

"Get misplaced, did you?"

The young man nodded. "Once or twice. Lost a lot of

time. Too much. Matter of fact, that's what I wanted to ask you about. Storekeeper said you're headed for Cunningham's. Wondered if I could ride along."

The old man studied him for a moment, then nodded. "Don't see why not." He held out his hand. "Rufe Kitrel."

The young man took his hand. "Lake Mattick. How long'll it take?"

Rufe pulled the horses' heads up from the water. "Two, three days. You in a hurry?"

The young man blinked. "No. Just . . . curious." He shrugged, but Rufe read a darkness in the young man's eyes that made him uneasy.

Frowning to himself, Rufe shook his head. Gettin' old, he thought, and turned toward the barn.

"Well, we'll be there in a couple, three days. Depends."

"Just as long as we get there." Lake nodded. "That's all that matters."

In the barn, Maggie Calder watched Rufe and the other man come back up from the corral and into the barn.

"This is Lake Mattick." Rufe introduced the man to the others, and Maggie realized it was the same man she'd seen coming out of the store earlier. "He'll be ridin' with us to Cunningham's," Rufe explained, then looked to Maggie. "That is if we go."

Maggie's throat tightened. "We're going, Mr. Kitrel," she said.

"Mrs. Calder, it looks like it might snow, and—"

"And it might not."

The muscles in the old man's jaw trembled in his beard, and Maggie could tell he didn't like being told what to do by a woman. Especially her.

"Mr. Kitrel," she softened her tone, "if I don't leave now, I'll just go some other time. I'd rather do it now."

The old man nodded. "All right," he said and looked at Dick Summers. "We packed?" Summers nodded.

"Then let's head out. Shorty—"

"Yeah."

"Get one of them pack animals."

Nodding, the small man turned up the aisle then stopped, staring into the stockade.

"Tim, you take the other, and I'll—"

He looked at Shorty.

"Shorty," he said, "I thought I tole you—"

"Look at this," the little man said, and the others came up beside him.

Maggie felt her breath catch when she saw what the little man was looking at. Indians. Five or six of them. Tall, clad in fur, their hair swept up in greased pompadours.

"Absoraka," Rufe said, and the Indians came by the barns. "Thought I smelled their smoke last night. Musta come down from the Leyenda."

Shorty walked the few steps to the door and stood looking disgustedly at them as they went by.

"Look at 'em," he sneered. "Ridin' in like anybody else."

"They come to trade," Rufe said. "That's what this place is for."

"They're killers," Shorty snapped. "Killed that fella up on the Mussellshell two months ago."

"Nobody knows that was Absoraka. These fellas are comin' in peaceful, just—"

"How 'bout him?" Shorty pointed to one brave with a rifle.

"One rifle in the whole bunch, don't make a war party. Now come on."

"All right." The little man nodded grudgingly, and turning back into the barn he spat in the Indians' direction.

As he did, one of the riders broke from the others. A boy, not more than thirteen, bolted toward the barn, then a second rider came after him, grasping the boy's reins, stopping him.

The second rider, a tall man on a roan horse, barked a few angry words at the boy, and the boy nodded sullenly, then turned his horse back to the others. The tall man remained, staring at the people in the barn.

"Boy's father," Rufe said, then looked at Shorty. "Get in there and get that horse."

"Goddammit, Rufe, he—"

"I said, get in there and get that horse, or I'm gonna reach down your throat and turn you inside out. Now move."

Trembling, the little man glared at Rufe for a moment, then pivoting, he stalked back into the barn.

Rufe looked back at the Indian and nodded. The Indian didn't respond. Instead, he turned his horse out and joined the others.

Rufe looked to Maggie. "Mrs. Calder," he said and

pointed to her horse, a small bay mare, "let's get this thing goin'."

Blinking, Maggie nodded. "Yes," she said. "Let's do that."

She walked to her horse and mounted up, her eyes moving back to the Indians. Her heart was beating so hard in her chest, she almost thought she could hear it. Rufe pulled his horse beside her.

"You all right, ma'am?"

"Yes." She nodded, and Rufe pulled out in front of her.

"Move out," he said.

Crossing the stockade, Maggie's eyes went back to the Indians dismounting in front of the store. It was as if there was nothing else in the stockade but them and her. She didn't know why, but Indians had always frightened her since she'd first seen them five years ago. Them and this land. Both held an unnamed fear for her.

They passed through the main gate of the stockade and she realized they were outside. Her eyes came around to see more Indians, maybe ten or fifteen, standing around a freshly built fire. Rufe came back alongside her.

"It's all right, ma'am. They'll do their tradin', then head back into the Leyenda."

"South?"

Rufe smiled. "Don't worry, ma'am. You'll never see'em. They don't like us any more'n we do them."

———◆———

Lake Mattick's eyes stayed with the Indians until they were past them, then turning front in the saddle, he put them out of his mind. Two or three days to Cunningham's, the old man had said.

The ex-soldier's hands tightened on the reins, and he nudged the Morgan out. Two or three days, he whispered to himself. Then it would be over.

CHAPTER 2

The party angled south down the barren hills, away from the mountains. Rufe was in the lead, then Dick Summers leading a pack horse, Maggie, Tim Carmody with the second pack horse, and Shorty bringing up the rear. Lake Mattick rode out to the side a little, alone.

The sun climbed higher in the sky and Maggie thought some heat would come, but it didn't. A steady breeze pushed down from the mountains chilling her.

The morning passed and they stopped for lunch behind

a hill out of the wind. After quickly eating a meal of cold meat and bread, they moved on.

In the saddle again, Maggie watched the hills ease by her, only to be replaced by more just like them, and she wondered how anybody could ride like this for any great length of time. Ordinarily she enjoyed riding and was good at it, but it was always done for just an hour or so. This was a little like being locked in a room with no walls.

The afternoon eased away, and Tim and Shorty carried on a spotty conversation, mostly having to do with horses, whiskey, times they had been drunk, and what they would do if they had the money.

Frowning, Maggie eased her horse out. She considered talking to the stranger, Mattick, then thought better of it. She didn't know him, and he didn't seem to want company. Pushing her horse around Dick Summers, she pulled in beside Rufe Kitrel.

The old man's eyes came around wonderingly. "Yes'um?"

Maggie smiled, shaking her head. "I wish I had a question to ask you, Mr. Kitrel. I don't. I'm just bored. Do you mind if I ride with you for a while?"

Rufe shrugged. "Suppose not," he allowed, then looked forward.

They came down a low hill and out onto a flat. Rufe's blue roan swung his head around to bite at a fly, and they moved on in silence.

Maggie smiled, nodding. "You're not enjoying this much are you?"

Kitrel frowned. "Not much, no ma'am. Just as soon be

doin' somethin' else, but you're dead set on it and your husband sort of volunteered us."

"He has a way of doing that," Maggie agreed. "I'm sorry you got stuck with the job."

The old man shrugged. "What comes of havin' a job, I reckon. What livin' on this damn prairie, scuse me, ma'am, will do to you."

"Why do you then?"

Rufe shrugged. "Make some for a stake so's me and old Dick can head back into the mountains," he explained, then frowned ruefully. "Course we been at it a while. Seems like somethin's always comin' up. Used to be fellas like me and Dick, the boys, companyeros would—"

"Companyeros?" Maggie asked.

Rufe looked at her. "What we called each other sometimes. From the Spanish. Means . . . well, friend, but more than that. Somebody you've been a ways with. . . ."

Maggie nodded and Rufe went on. "Anyhow, it used to be that we could trap all winter, sell the furs, have ourselves a hoot, then have enough left for supplies and go back to the mountains and do it again. But now the fur trade's gone to hell, scuse me, ma'am."

Maggie gazed at the mountains. "It's hard to believe anyone could live up there all the time."

"Why's that?"

Maggie's eyes came back. "I don't know." She shrugged. "Because they're so . . . wild. Uncontrollable, I guess."

Kitrel smiled, almost as if he were remembering a

woman. "That they are." He nodded. "That they are." He looked forward. "Now if you'll pardon me, ma'am, I'm gonna take a ride up and have a look-see."

"Why, do you think the Indians—?"

Rufe smiled. "No, ma'am. Just my way. I like to know what's around me 'fore I camp. Even if it's nothin'."

"Thank you for the conversation."

"Hardly no pain at all."

"You . . . don't sound quite as angry with me anymore."

Rufe looked at her, his eyes shadowing slightly. "Never was mad at you, Mrs. Calder. Just that when somebody gives their word, they oughta keep it."

"Sometimes it's not as simple as that."

"Your word is your word, ma'am. To me, it is as simple as that. Scuse me," he said and nudged his horse out.

Maggie watched him, then closed her eyes for a moment. "I wish it were, Mr. Kitrel," she whispered and opened them again. "I only wish it were."

———————◆———————

Out to the side, Lake Mattick watched the old man spur his roan and move out. Stretching restlessly in the saddle, he wished there had been another way of doing this. But there wasn't. Kitrel knew the country and he didn't, and the one thing Lake didn't need right now was another delay.

He looked up at the sky. The first hues of twilight were beginning. It would be dark in another two hours. He nodded. With any luck they would get to Cunningham's in another two days. Not long now, he thought. Not long.

They made camp in a cottonwood grove, on the banks of a small stream. Sitting next to the fire, Lake poured himself another cup of coffee and leaned back on his saddle. Across from him Rufe Kitrel lit up his pipe and perfumed the air with great draughts of tobacco. The woman was down by the creek, sitting alone by the water, her eyes toward the mountains. Dick Summers and Shorty were tending the horses. Tim Carmody was prone on the ground, already asleep.

Beside the creek, the woman stood up and came back to the fire, a shadow in the fluttering light.

Lake smiled at her as she knelt down, taking the handle of the coffee pot. He hadn't really taken note of her until they camped. The proximity of the fire and the ring of darkness around them made everything touched by the light seem closer.

She was not a beautiful woman, but there was something about her that held his eyes. A wing of her dark hair came loose as she poured the coffee, and the smoke and light blended around her. Her eyes came up and Lake realized he was staring at her.

Smiling awkwardly, he nodded. "Mrs. Calder."

"Yes?"

"I . . . understand you're headed east," he said because he couldn't think of anything else to say.

"That's right." She nodded. "Albany."

"Nice town."

"Have you been there?"

"Once, yes'um. During the war. Goin' for a visit?"

Her eyes darkened, and it took her a moment to answer. "No," she finally said. "I'm going to divorce my husband." Taking her coffee, she stood up. "Goodnight, Mr. Mattick."

"Ma'am." He nodded and watched her walk back down to the creek.

He glanced at Rufe and cocked his head. "Guess I put my foot in it."

The old mountain man grinned. "Reckon you did." He pointed at Lake's rifle in the boot next to the saddle and the saber. "Just noticin' your piece. Cartridge?"

Lake nodded and reached around; he pulled it from its scabbard and handed it to Rufe. The old hunter rolled it in his hands like a shard of jewelry.

"Called a Henry," Lake explained. "Holds sixteen shots—"

The old hunter looked up. "Sixteen, damn—"

Lake smiled. "Course it's a bitch to load. Magazine's there on the bottom. Got to uncap it and drop the shells in."

As Rufe looked at it, Shorty and Dick walked in. They knelt down in front of the fire, and Rufe handed the rifle to Dick.

"Sure are makin' things easy," Dick sighed and handed it to Shorty. "Good weapon to have out here," he said, then nodded to Mattick's saber. "More'n that thing."

"Yeah." Shorty grinned, giving the rifle back to Lake. "'Bout the only thing that'll be good for is frog stickin'."

"It's come in handy before," Mattick replied curtly.

"Never seen one," Shorty said. "Mind if I look at it?" And he reached for it.

Mattick stopped his hand. "Yes," he said. "I do."

Shorty sat back, his face flushing. "Listen," he growled tightly, his fist gathering, and Rufe laughed. The little man swung around, staring at him.

"Shorty," he sighed, "ever occur to you there are some things personal to a fella?"

"Well, he don't have—"

"How else would he've said it?"

Shorty blinked, the flush in his face deepening.

"He still coulda been more polite about it," he snapped and, standing, he walked to his bedroll and lay down.

Rufe shook his head. "Easiest man to rile I ever seen," he said and looked at Lake. "But he was right; you coulda been a little more hospitable."

"That's something I haven't been concerned with for a while."

"Yeah." Rufe frowned. "That set-to back east. Hear tell they tried to make war a way of life."

"They didn't just try," Lake said and leaned back into his saddle, pulling the blanket up over him.

Rufe started to say something more, then shrugging, he turned to his blanket instead.

Rolling onto his side, Lake saw the woman down by the creek. He watched her for a moment, then closed his eyes. A long time later, he thought he heard her come back up the hill.

CHAPTER 3

Beneath her blankets, Maggie Calder was dreaming. She was on a vast plain. Alone. Turning, there were mountains behind her, and a deep forest. In the trees, she could hear something moving toward her. Running. Smashing limbs and bushes as it came. Plunging toward her. Yet she couldn't see it. She tried to turn. To run. But she couldn't. All she could do was stand and listen to it coming.

Suddenly there was a pressure on her shoulder. Shaking her. Reeling, she flailed against it and awakened to see a dark form hovering above her. She hit against his hand, trying to get away.

"Mrs. Calder," he said, and blinking she realized it was Rufe.

"You all right, ma'am?"

Trembling, she nodded and sat up and felt snow against her face. Looking up, she saw a shroud of it over them. Everything was white. There was no longer a plain or mountains. Only the gaunt forms of the cottonwoods around them. And the hovering white.

"Time to be movin', ma'am," the old man said. "Gonna have to find some better shelter. It's comin' down pretty hard."

She pushed her blankets aside. "Is there coffee?"

"No time," the old man answered. "Liable to blizzard on us."

Her eyes jerked up. "We're not going back."

The old man frowned. "No, ma'am. Too far. Canyon near here. It'll do us till this lets up." He stood up. "Try to hurry, ma'am."

Saddling his Morgan, Lake watched the old man as he crossed from the woman to his blue roan.

"Remind me not to doubt you again," he said.

The old man glanced up at the sky. "Worse'n I figured. Canyon not far from here. Only shelter I know of out here. It'll do us till it blows over."

Lake frowned. "How long?"

Rufe looked at him. "What?"

"How long you think we'll be delayed?"

"Damn, lieutenant, you are in a hurry ain't you? What you got waitin' up there, a woman or money?"

Lake's eyes darkened. "Neither."

The old man gazed at him, then nodded knowingly. "Yeah," he said. "Well, it's gonna be a while." He turned to the others readying their animals. Summers was the nearest to be finished. "Dick," he called, "when you get done, help the woman. Tim, how's that pack animal?"

The red-haired youth nodded. "All right. Little skittish."

The old man turned to his horse. "Well, let's hurry it up and get the hell out of here."

Summers helped the woman with her bedroll, and Carmody finished with his pack horse.

Mounting up, Rufe led them out into the blind curtain of white, pushing down into a draw, then up the bank, climbing the hill on the opposite side. Stretching out into single file, they crested the hill and angled down it, through a small valley, then out along what seemed to be a thrust of hills.

The figures in front of Lake began to blur, hovering, slowly whispering away from him. Caught between two places, neither of them defined. Lake glanced up and around. Visibility was down to less than twenty feet. Swearing softly, he shook his head. It was getting worse.

———◆———

Ahead of Lake, Maggie's hands tightened on her saddle horn, and she half wished they hadn't come at all. Maybe she should have waited. Frowning, she shook her head. That would have just been putting it off. It was foolish to be afraid, she knew that, but the dream she'd had that morning was still vivid in her mind and stomach. Like something scrawled with fire.

She looked up and around. Once she had loved the snow. In Albany. In her childhood. In the soft days when snow meant laughter, fortresses, and sleds. And a boy named Nathaniel Finch.

During her last two years in high school, he had been all she thought of. She could still remember the first time he'd kissed her. They were walking home in the snowfall after skating at the pond, hurrying along a path through a gathering of winter-dead sycamore and elm, when he put his hand out taking her arm. Turning her.

They bumped noses as his lips pushed against hers, and she almost laughed. Then his hand slipped up her side, cupping her breast. She felt her breath rush, then stepped back away from him, leaving his hand awkwardly poised in the air.

Blinking, she stared at him for a moment, then kissing him quickly, she turned and ran. She ran all the way home and thought about him and the feeling of being against him for the rest of the day and into the night.

She smiled with the memory of him and his hand poised in the air. She might have married him, she thought, then the smile was whispered away. No. There had never been a chance of that. He was not their kind of people, her parents had said. There were certain ways of doing things. . . .

"Canyon," Rufe called, and her eyes jerked up.

Ahead of her she could see rock walls pushing out of the snow-mist toward them. Relaxing, she tried to think of Nathaniel again, then realized with a tightening of her hands on the saddle horn that he and that time were gone. They had been for a long time.

———◆———

Lake watched the canyon walls ease up around them like gray fluid. Pressing toward them, pulling them down, then slipping back away into the snowfall. Rufe led them downward. Across an open area, then the walls were there again.

Ahead, Lake saw Rufe turn a curve in the rock. Then the others. As he neared it, Mattick could make out another open clearing—

Then he heard the shout. It was Kitrel. And somebody else. Spurring his horse hard, Lake charged around the corner and into the clearing.

At first he couldn't see anything except that the clearing was a large one. Then deep into it, through the curtain of snow, he saw the figures on the ground.

Men.

His breath hit his chest like a hammer, and he blinked, stunned. The men on the ground were Indians. A lot of them. All over the place. He and the others had ridden right down into their camp.

"Holy . . ." Lake whispered and automatically jerked the Henry from its scabbard. In front of him, it was a labyrinth of confusion and movement. Like someone dropping a puzzle. Ragged pieces exploding everywhere.

Summers' horse was rearing and he'd lost his pack animal. Carmody's pack horse was backing, tearing at its reins. Shorty was drawing his rifle. Maggie had spurred her bay, and Rufe was wheeling his blue, shouting to the others.

"I said run for it," he screamed, then strapped his horse, coming alongside Maggie, turning, and they both rode for the far side of the clearing.

Carmody flung away his pack animal's rope and followed them.

Shorty's rifle came free.

Dick Summers' horse rose up on its hind legs, screaming and turning at the same time, beginning to pitch over backward. Dick kicked away from the horse, trying to come down on his feet, but the momentum of the animal was still with him and he crashed down on his back, catching his right foot under him, smashing it with his own weight.

Kicking his Morgan, Lake plunged through the swarm of Indians to him.

"Summers," Lake shouted.

The old man's eyes came up, his cap slipping off, his bald head gleaming. Next to him, his horse was already up and running. Shoving himself to his feet, Dick started to chase him, but his foot gave way under him.

Lake swept his horse into the bald-headed man, reining the animal, and Dick pushed himself up again, grasping the pommel of Lake's saddle.

"Haul it," Dick ordered him, and Lake turned the Morgan out, strapping him and giving him his head.

On the edge of his vision, he could see Shorty. His rifle coming up. On the ground, an Indian was charging the little man. It was the Absoraka boy he had seen at Calder's. There was a knife in his hand.

"Shorty— No—" he screamed. The sound of his voice mixed with the crash of Shorty's rifle, and the Indian boy's head shattered as the slug slammed him into the snow.

Behind the boy, his father emerged from the snowfall, running to his son, then kneeling beside him, the grief stark on his face.

Turning, Shorty ran.

"Goddammit," Lake growled, then remembered Dick hanging from his saddle.

"Keep goin'," the bald-headed man barked.

Lake kicked the horse out, then shifted the Henry to his rein hand and reached down, burying his free hand in Dick's coat, and pulled. The bald-headed man inched up slowly, dragging himself over the Morgan's back with Lake's help.

They hammered across the clearing, through the Indians, and began to leave them behind. Summers hooked his knee over the Morgan and, lifting himself, he slipped his leg over and sat up behind Lake. A shot crashed and Lake felt the ball cut the air beside them.

"One of'em's got a rifle," Summers shouted, and Lake strapped the Morgan hard, guiding him between two trees, then saw the canyon walls coming up again.

"How we doin' back there?" he asked Dick.

The bald-headed man turned. "They're comin'," he reported.

"Fast?"

"Couple. One with the rifle's still on the ground. Reloadin'."

They plunged into the cut between the walls, and Lake had to slow the Morgan to keep from hurdling into the rock face. Twenty yards down the channel, Lake could make out Rufe, Maggie, Carmody, and Shorty waiting. Rufe waved his arm for them to hurry, then turned, pushing his horse out.

Lake followed, all of them clattering over broken rock. He came around a hard twist in the rock, pounded through an ice-crusted stream, then felt his horse pulling upward. The walls began to fall away, and coming around a bend the walls were gone completely. Above him on a crest, he could see the others reining in. Turning. Lake came up beside them, wheeling his horse around.

"You all right?" Rufe asked Summers.

The bald-headed man frowned. "Twisted my foot."

"Will it hold you?"

"Ain't tried it yet."

Rufe looked to the woman. "Mrs. Calder—" Maggie nodded.

"How good are you on a horse?"

"I've been riding all my life—" Her eyes went back to the canyon mouth. "Shouldn't we be—?"

"In a bit." Kitrel nodded. "Right now we need to slow'em a bit—"

"Rufe—" Tim barked.

Below them, an Indian burst from the mouth of the canyon.

"Hold it," Rufe said slowly and cocked his Hawken. The Indian hammered toward them.

"Wouldn't wait too long," Dick said. "One of 'em's got a rifle."

"They're the ones from the fort, and I only saw the one piece there."

"He'll still have range."

Another figure charged from the canyon, and swearing, Rufe raised his Hawken. "Dick's right," he barked. "Fire."

The rifles spasmed a line of fire, and the Indian in the lead twisted off his horse, but the others kept coming, and more poured from the canyon as Rufe and his men dropped their rifles down to reload.

Levering the Henry, Mattick fired again. Then again. Pumping and firing fifteen times until the rifle was empty, the lead spraying over the rocks and the canyon opening like a holocaust, turning the charging Indians. A thick silence hovered in the wake of the gunfire.

"Damn . . ." Tim Carmody swallowed, staring at the Henry.

"Let's get out of here," Rufe said. "That surprised 'em. Next time they'll expect it."

"Maybe we could hold 'em in there," Shorty put in.

"No cover," Rufe countered. "'Sides there are other ways out of that canyon." He turned his horse. "No cover anywhere out here."

"The South Fork," Dick suggested.

"The river?" Rufe said. "How far you think?"

"Four, five miles."

"Yeah." Rufe nodded. "We might just pull it off. Let's move," he shouted, and swinging his horse out, he strapped him hard.

CHAPTER 4

They ran. Over the rise and out onto a flat that lay before them like a great white table. Stringing out in a line, they cut across the snow. Rufe in the lead. Then Maggie, Carmody, Shorty, and Mattick and Summers. The snow was well up over the horses' hooves, and Rufe pushed into it hard, driving his blue roan.

Glancing back, Lake looked at the swath they were leaving in the snow, then raising his eyes, he saw the blur of Indians topping the rise and descending darkly toward them. Behind him, Dick was looking back too. His eyes came around to Mattick's.

"We got about five minutes on'em," the bald-headed man gauged.

Lake nodded his agreement, then turning forward, he saw that Kitrel and the others were gaining on him slightly. A knot thickened in his stomach and he strapped the Morgan, but the snow and weight were slowing them.

"I'm weightin' you down," Summers said, voicing Lake's thoughts.

Lake smiled guiltily. "I like the company."

"Trouble is," Summers pointed out, "this brand of friendly might get you killed."

Lake nodded. "I'll just have to stay ahead of 'em."

Lake strapped the Morgan, and they gained a little on the others, hammering across the cold ground, then began to lose it again slowly. Beneath him, Lake could feel the Morgan straining to keep up, his breath pounding through him, condensing in short ragged spurts, and could tell he was weakening.

In the lead, Rufe looked back once. Then again. Swinging his horse out, he started back toward the rear.

"Keep goin'," he shouted to Maggie and wheeled in beside Lake and Dick, bringing his horse in parallel, then right next to the Morgan.

"Get aboard," he barked at Dick.

The bald-headed man's eyes darted back, then to Rufe. Swallowing, he nodded. The horses were running in stride now. Down a small drop and up again.

Bringing his knee up, Summers shoved it between him and the Morgan, then reached out with his right hand to

Rufe and balanced himself against Lake with his left. They slammed down another sink, and Dick's hand gripped Lake's coat hard, jerking against him, tipping them both outward. Clutching the pommel, Lake kept himself in the saddle, and Dick maintained his balance.

"Jesus," Lake heard the bald-headed man whisper thickly.

Lake eased the Morgan gently in to Rufe until the horses were in stride again. The snow whorled into Lake's eyes, but he kept the horse in line. Behind him, he knew Dick was hesitating.

"Dick," Rufe urged him.

And the bald-headed man moved. Shoving off Lake, jacking his left leg, and swinging the right, hurdling himself into the air, and over Rufe's roan, slamming into the horse's rump. Landing. Catching hold of Rufe's saddle. Screaming a bark of pain as he jammed the twisted foot into the blue's side. But he held on. His fingers dug into the saddle. The pain cording the blood vessels in his face and over the naked skin of his scalp.

"Dick?" Rufe asked.

"I'm with you," Summers growled.

Lake edged his horse away from them, and Rufe pulled in front slightly. Beneath him Lake could nearly feel the relief in the horse, but he was still tired.

Glancing back, he squinted trying to see the Indians, but the snowfall masked them away, hiding them. But they were coming, he knew that. Pressing toward them.

Lake's eyes moved up and around. The curtain of white had become something living in the Indians. Something hostile. A part of the enemy. He looked forward at the others. Shadows now. Reduced to form and movement. Plunging blindly into the white.

Suddenly a draw yawned in front of them. They dropped into it, then started up the other bank.

"River," Rufe shouted. "That way"—he pointed into the snow—"'bout a mile."

Lake felt the hope burst through him like a rush of hot water. Charging out of the draw, they skirted the base of a hill, hammering through rocks, then through the gaunt scrawl of piñon. Then the river.

In the lead, Maggie, Shorty, and Carmody reined up on the bank and waited for Rufe, Dick, and Lake to catch up with them. Rufe hauled his horse in and looked at the stream. There was some ice, but the water was still running.

"Upstream," he said and plunged his horse into the water.

The others followed, clamoring into the hoof-deep water, echoing spray into the white, freezing air. Fragments of wet cut across Lake's face, shocking him, bringing feeling back into his skin.

They came into a grove of pine and aspen. Rufe turned his horse out, pushing toward the middle of the stream to avoid hitting the limbs. Anything broken would leave a trail.

The water deepened, edging up the Morgan's legs, but Lake kept him moving. Off to his side the bank ebbed away in the snowfall, leaving only water and the memory of land and form.

Rufe led them across the river, and to within five feet of the opposite bank, but he stayed in the water. Following the shadowed outline of the bank, Rufe found shallower water and strapped his horse out.

They moved upward. Gradually. Slowly. Too damn slow. Around rocks and over downed logs. Lake wanted to get the hell out of the water and onto the bank and run again, but he knew he couldn't. That would kill him quicker than anything.

The river narrowed between rising banks, and the water deepened again, gliding up around the horses' legs, gaining in current. The bed steepened under them suddenly, and Lake could feel the Morgan fighting the water and the incline.

Rufe's horse stumbled, but the old mountain man brought his horse's head up, helping him keep his footing.

"I'm gonna take us both down," Summers said behind him.

"Shut up," Rufe whispered evenly and spurred his horse on.

"Dammit, Rufe—"

"Not now," Rufe snapped, the patience gone out of his voice, and he spurred his roan again and strapped him, forcing him up the stream.

The horses struggled against the current, their hooves slipping on the smooth rocks of the riverbed. Their breath raked through them, raw, mixing with the rasp of the men's desperate breathing.

Shorty strapped his horse angrily. "You son-of-a-bitch," he whisper-screamed.

Carmody was talking to his animal, quietly, assuredly. The woman was working her horse gently, patting his neck and whispering to him, nearly prayerlike, white words, mingling with the other sounds, honing an edge to the air, putting a smell in it.

Trembling, Lake looked forward. The river stretched up into the snowfall.

"Hup," he whispered to the Morgan and they pulled upward, following Rufe. They came around a house-sized boulder jutting from the bank, then weaved through a morass of driftwood, then up again. Into the white.

"Jesus," Tim whispered. "How long's this gorge go for—?"

Rufe didn't answer. He kept moving.

"Rufe—?"

"I don't know," the old hunter growled his answer pushing his roan harder. Up a small falls, and around another narrow bend. The water ebbed back, shallowing, and the old hunter spurred his horse, nearly running him.

Lake nudged his Morgan out, falling in behind Rufe and Dick. The river straightened and flattened in front of them, and they cut the water into plumes hammering over smooth stones. They had run nearly half a mile when the walls of the gorge began to ease back, blending into the snow, the gaunt shapes of pine and aspen taking their place.

"We're out of it," Carmody whispered.

Wordlessly, Rufe turned his roan up the bank and out of the water, guiding him between the trees. The trunks whispered by, flickering silently behind, then suddenly Rufe pulled up, his eyes swinging back, fixing intently on the river and the rattle of the running water as if he were watching the sound.

Lake reined up, looking back too, thinking the old man

might have heard something. He listened for a moment, then looked to Rufe questioningly.

"The gorge." The old man nodded before Lake could say anything, then spurred his horse out back toward the river.

Maggie came up behind Lake, watching Rufe. "He's going back," she said incredulously. "Why is he going back?"

"I don't know," Lake said, strapping his horse, "but I'm going to find out."

CHAPTER 5

Lake caught up with Rufe and Dick, as they pushed back down to the river, then turned paralleling the bank, back the way they'd come.

"Rufe, you mind—?" Lake said.

"Not now." The old man shook his head, and they climbed the slope where the gorge began, then topped the crest at a run. The trees thinned, then were gone, falling away into the snow, and they eased over to the rim of the gorge, slowing their horses to a trot, then to a walk.

Rufe skirted the edge, his eyes intently searching into

the white whorling space below. Following Rufe's gaze, Lake could barely make out the motion of the water through the trembling of white.

"Here." The old man nodded and pulled away from the side and reined in his horse. Swinging his leg over his horse's neck, he slipped the other foot from the stirrup and dropped to the ground, and Lake dismounted as Rufe helped Dick from the roan.

"How's the foot?" Rufe asked the bald-headed man. "Busted, you figger?"

Summers winced slightly, standing on his good foot and supporting himself against the blue roan.

"Likely," he allowed tightly, the cords of his neck tautening like old rope.

Nodding, Rufe looked up as Carmody, Shorty, and Maggie rode in behind them. Lake came around his horse.

"Rufe," he said, "you mind telling me what the hell's going on?"

The old hunter rubbed his nose. "Gonna bushwhack'em," he answered, then looked at the other men. "Shorty, you and Tim dismount and go on down a piece. Let me know when they're comin'—"

"Bushwhack?" Lake asked incredulously. "You mean wait for them? Dammit, Rufe, we're ahead—"

"Shorty"—the old hunter cut him off—"you and Tim do like I told you."

"Listen, Rufe," Shorty said standing down, "maybe, he's right—"

"Shorty," the old hunter growled, "if you hadn't snapped off that shot, we wouldn't be in this."

"They—"

"They, hell. They just come from tradin' back at the post. Musta gone down that canyon to get out of the storm and thought we'd come to rob'em."

Shorty looked at the others. "He had a knife," he said. "I—"

"I know." Rufe frowned, and his voice softened. "I know. . . ."

"But to ambush them," Maggie said, dismounting. "In cold blood—"

"Mrs. Calder," the old man answered tightly, "I don't like it any better'n you do. I never bushwhacked a man in my life. But we don't have any choice anymore. A boy was killed back there. A man's son. And likely he thinks we were thieves. That makes us all responsible. Nothin' we could say or do's gonna make any difference to him. All he wants is us dead, and he'll chase us into hell if he has to. Game's been dealt, now we got to play it out." He looked to Tim and Shorty. "You boys get goin'."

Tim dismounted and handed Maggie his reins. Shorty hesitated a moment, then gave Maggie his leathers, and he and Tim ran into the snowfall. Rufe watched them for a moment, then bringing his Hawken up, he began reloading.

Frowning, Lake approached the old hunter again. "Rufe, listen—"

"We ain't got the time, lieutenant. You'd better get to loadin' that piece—"

"Dammit, that's just the point. We do have the time. We might outrun them to Cunningham's—"

"Ain't goin' to Cunningham's."

Lake blinked. "Then where—?"

"Place I mentioned before. New Eden. Closer. We'll outnumber'em then, and maybe they'll give it up. Then we can get to Cunningham's. But we ain't even gonna get to New Eden unless we hurt those Absoraka and hurt'em bad, and this is the only chance we got at it."

"Rufe—"

"Dammit, shut up and listen. They've likely split tryin' to pick up our sign. Some have come after us, the rest have gone downstream. That puts the odds a little in our favor and we got to take it. Here we got cover and an out. We get out on that goddamn prairie again and there ain't no way we can fight'em and get away. There's no cover. We hit'em now, and we can slow'em. Kill them and their horses."

Lake shook his head. "You're gamblin', Rufe. You don't know that they'll split. And you don't know they'll come up the stream after us. They all might have gone the other way. Our best bet is the run for Cunningham's."

"Bullshit," the old hunter growled. "We're dead for sure that way. And you're right, I am gamblin', but that's the only way out of this." His eyes narrowed. "Thought you officered in that war— Hell, boy, didn't you ever take a gamble?"

Lake blinked. "I followed orders," he said. "And didn't take unnecessary chances."

"And I'll bet all your boys come through it without a scratch."

Lake's eyes darkened. "No," he whispered. "Most of them are dead."

The silent pad of feet silenced them and Rufe turned, raising his Hawken. Tim Carmody materialized from the snowfall.

"They're comin'," he whispered.

Rufe nodded and asked, "How many?"

"Didn't see'em." Carmody shivered. "Just heard'em. They're maybe five minutes back."

Rufe turned. "Mrs. Calder, I'd get down if I were you. Dick—"

"I'll keep an eye on the horses," the bald-headed man said.

Rufe turned back to Carmody. "Get back to where you were," he said. "Let'em get between us 'fore you start firin'. And, Tim—"

"Yessir?"

"Get that one with the rifle first, if he's down there and if you can."

Nodding, Carmody ran back into the snowfall, and Rufe looked at Lake.

"That goes for you too. Now I'd get that thing loaded. We're runnin' out of time," he snapped and turned toward the gorge.

Lake stared after the old man for a moment, then frowning, he walked to his horse. Opening his saddlebags, he took out a belt with a knife and a large cartridge box strung on it. Kneeling down, he unlatched the brass stud at the bottom of the box and lifted the heavy leather flap. Inside there had been separate compartments for cleaning equipment, powder, and balls, but Lake had taken it all out and used it now just for the Henry ammunition.

He had a good supply left, he nodded as he took out a handful of the shells and began loading the rifle through its bottom barrel.

When he was finished, Lake closed and latched the box, then strung the belt around his waist, buckled it, checked the tie on the knife, and stood up. Through the snowfall, he could see the vague outline of the old man lying on the crest above the gorge.

The muscles in Lake's jaw hardened.

"Damn," he growled shaking his head, then hurried toward the gorge.

CHAPTER 6

Edging up to the rim, Lake picked a spot about six feet away from Rufe, then knelt down in the snow and stretched out flat on his belly. He looked into the gorge below him; the wind rustled the snowfall. Touching it like a melody without sound. Filling the ravine with gray echoes and silence.

Lake eased his breath through his raw lungs, thinking about it, rhythming himself calm. It was a reflex now, he thought; he'd done it so many times before, waiting—

He trembled slightly and swallowed, fighting a knot of

panic twisting in his throat. He was waiting again. Hiding again. And it was as if he'd never moved. Never traveled. Never ridden the long miles between Tennessee and wherever he was now. As if he'd run a circle in time. Back to where he'd been. Repeating his motion, becoming an echo of himself. Muscles tautening. Eyes straining. Fingers hovering on the rifle, coldness spread through his armpits, crotch, and the backs of his hands.

Waiting. It seemed as if he had always been waiting but could never remember it afterward as if it carried its own amnesia.

A flicker in the gorge drew his eyes. The barrel of the Henry nosed to it automatically. The movement became a smear of brown, weaving itself from the white, gaining form. Drifting under Rufe, Lake could see him more clearly now. An Indian. Fur-clad.

More figures materialized out of the snowfall, and Lake hurriedly moved his eyes over their blurred outlines, trying to pick out a rifle barrel. The man with the rifle was the one they needed to kill first.

The gorge filled with the men and the sound of their ponies' hooves rattling against the stones, but Lake could see no sign of the rifle anywhere. The man with the rifle had likely gone downstream with the other half of the party. Swearing softly, Lake strained his eyes. He wanted that man now instead of later. Now, it was on Lake's terms. Later, it would be on the Indian's.

Frowning, the ex-soldier gave it up and looked back to the man in the lead. The Indian was passing directly under Lake, dark eyes scanning the bank.

Lake moved his gaze from the man's face. He didn't want to know what the Indian looked like. Lake had

killed a lot of men. So many that he had stopped counting. He had to. And he had never seen their faces. He
remembered them only by form and place. They were the
enemy, not individuals, none of them real, because he'd
never seen their faces.

The man in the lead pushed beyond Lake, and in one
movement the ex-soldier slipped the Henry into his shoulder, sighted down on the broadest part of the Indian's
back, and squeezed the trigger, letting the hammer fall.

The crash of the shot scattered the snow-quiet. The
slug smashed through the brave's back pitching him forward, but Lake didn't wait to watch him fall. Levering
the Henry, he went to work.

Down the rim, he could hear the roar of Rufe, Tim, and
Shorty's Hawkens. Lake swung his rifle, picking his shots,
gauging three in advance, so he could fire with a mini-
mum of wasted movement.

He dropped a second brave, then one behind him,
sending them both sprawling into the freezing water at
the same time.

Still moving, levering the Henry again, Lake beaded
down on a man on a spotted pony, firing just as the Indian reeled his animal toward the bank.

"Damn," Lake growled, missing, levering the Henry.

The brave tumbled over the opposite side of his horse,
holding onto the animal's mane. Mattick felt himself hesi-
tate, then fired putting a slug through the pony's head,
kicking him around, hurling the brave off into the water.
Rolling, the brave pushed himself up, getting his feet
under him, and Lake shot him, blasting him back in the
water.

The whine of an arrow split the air inside him. Another

struck in the bank below him. Down from him, the Hawkens were sounding again.

Lake pumped three more shots into the gorge, firing at anything that moved, momentum rather than logic pushing him now. Then below him, he saw one of the braves charging the steep bank, pushing his horse, a small roan pony. Lake recognized the horse first, then the man.

It was the dead boy's father. Strapping the roan, the Indian ran the animal until he was nearly on his knees, clawing at the rock and dirt.

Blinking, Lake squeezed off a shot before he really beaded. He missed, but the crash of the shot frightened the roan and, rearing, the horse threw the brave off, then reeled, tumbling down the slope.

Off to the side the boy's father pulled himself out of the snow, dragging his eyes up to Lake's. Levering his rifle, Lake hesitated, staring at the man's face for a split second, then realized what he had done. But the brave was already moving, pushing himself up, hurling himself to one side, tumbling down the incline, smashing through the snow, toward a cut in the bank.

Lake fired, blasting the snow and dirt behind the running man. Then another as the brave plummeted into the cut and to cover.

"Dammit," Lake growled, but felt a curious relief. Ignoring it, he swung his rifle back to the river. The rest of the Indians were retreating, running their horses back down the stream, around a bend, and to cover. Lake fired after them but couldn't get a clear shot.

As the last of the Absorakas rounded the turn, the ex-soldier lowered his rifle and looked into the gorge. It was hard to tell how many they had killed. The bodies of the men and horses were mixed together. Strewn about like something a madman would dream. Five, he thought. Maybe six.

"Jesus . . ." he murmured and, trembling, he closed his eyes. The hurried pad of running feet pulled them open again. Rufe and the others were making for the horses.

Lake looked into the gorge again, then backing away, he turned and ran.

CHAPTER 7

Maggie held her hands to her ears, trying to close out the
roar of the shots and the screaming of men and horses,
but it had done no good. The sound of it seeped through
her like audible blood. There wasn't even a direction to it.
It seemed to be all around her, echoing in the snow. Then
it was silent.

Her eyes fixed in the direction of the gorge, thinking
the Indians might come for her any minute. Rushing at
her—Suddenly men were there. Plunging out of the snow.

Running. She bolted up, then saw it was Rufe. And Lake Mattick.

Rufe ran past her and helped Summers who was already struggling to his feet. Lake joined him and he and Rufe pushed the bald-headed man up on Kitrel's blue, and Shorty and Carmody charged in.

Maggie stood staring at the men as they swung into their saddles, then someone was pushing her toward her own horse. It was Lake. Ramming her into her animal. Then lifting her up.

"I can do it," she snapped.

"Then do it," Lake growled and turned to his Morgan and swung up into the saddle. Then reeling the horse out, he slapped Maggie's animal on the rear. And they were running again.

Rufe led them away from the gorge, then cut sharply back to the trees where they'd come out of the river. Crossing his own trail, he rode out in a wide half circle and headed back downstream, running the horses hard. They pushed out onto flat ground and Rufe pulled his horse in.

"Rest'em a minute," he called and the others pulled in beside him, except for Mattick. He rode wide and a little behind.

"Anyone get the one with the rifle?" Rufe asked.

"Don't think he was there," Lake said.

"Yeah." The old man frowned. "I didn't see him either. But, we'll hear from him later."

"Damn," Carmody sighed, grinning. "We hit'em though, didn't we?" He stretched his back. "Glad we can finally take it easy—"

"Not takin' it easy," the old man cut in. "These animals

are tired. That stop back there wasn't enough for'em. Can't push a saddle horse like you can those team animals. You ought to know that."

"Yeah," Carmody agreed and looked back again. "Just that—"

"Just nothin'," the old man growled. "We slowed and hurt'em. Killed six or seven. Maybe got a little of a lead. But they're still comin'. Them that was downstream, and them we dehorsed. Them on foot are holdin' on to the other's horses' tails, runnin' behind. And they'll run till they drop. They all will if they have to."

"Hell, why don't they—?" Carmody began, then swallowed, avoiding Dick Summer's eyes.

The bald-headed man smiled. "They don't ride double because they know that'll tire a horse quicker'n anything."

"Sorry." Carmody frowned. "I wasn't thinkin'."

"That's what makes you so amiable, Tim-boy," Dick grinned. "You got a mouth that don't wait for its brain. Now, if you don't mind company for a while, I think I'll hitch along behind you."

"Dick—" Rufe protested.

"Rufe," Summers sighed, "the last time you and me got into it, it was a draw, so you might as well save yourself the time and trouble."

Rufe stared at him a moment. "You know somethin'—"

"Yeah." Summers nodded. "I'm a hardheaded old bossloper."

"First time I ever knew you to be right," Rufe growled and eased his horse over to Carmody's, bringing him in parallel.

Leaning over Dick reached out, caught the back of

Carmody's saddle, and pulled himself over. Rufe could see the pain whiten his face and hear his breathing thin, but the bald-headed old man eased to the other horse's rump without saying anything. Frowning, Rufe spurred his horse out.

———————◄◆►———————

Lake watched the transfer and felt himself staring at Summers. A dead man, he nodded, then tried to push the thought from his head, as if his thinking it would make it come true. Turning his horse out, he noticed that Maggie Calder's horse had slowed nearly to a stop, and she was looking back into the snowfall as if she were hypnotized by the pale movement. An uneasiness razored his stomach. He had seen that look before. In the war. In the eyes of men about to break. Nudging his horse out, he angled in beside her.

"Mrs. Calder." Her eyes hovered on the snow.

His voice hardened. "Mrs. Calder."

Maggie's eyes jerked to his, startled, gazing at him as if he were a stranger.

"You all right, ma'am?"

She nodded stiffly. "I just—" She swallowed and shook her head.

Lake frowned. He wished now, he hadn't done this. He wanted to turn his horse out and away, but knew that she needed someone to talk to, at least for a few minutes. He had done it before, out of duty. He could do it one more time. If he didn't, she would slow them even more.

"You just what, Mrs. Calder?"

She looked at him, then at the others. "They're all such nice men. . . ."

"Ma'am?"

"They're all such nice men," she said again, pulling her eyes back to his. "And I'm afraid . . . if it weren't for me, they wouldn't be out here."

Lake shook his head. "You didn't know what was going to happen. You can't stay in one place because you're afraid of what'll happen goin' to another."

"No," Maggie acknowledged quietly. "I couldn't have stayed there any longer."

They rode for a few steps, then Lake asked, "What'd he do? Your husband, I mean."

Maggie looked at him. "That's the funny part of it. Nothing really."

"You left him for nothin'?"

"No." She shook her head. "It's hard to explain." She thought for a moment. "When I was about six, my father made a swing in the yard. When he put me in it, he pushed me and I went up in the air. At first it was fun. But then I kept going higher and higher, and my father kept pushing. I remember I wanted to scream. But I couldn't. I was so frightened, I couldn't do anything, even cry. And I kept going higher. I wanted to do something, but there was nothing I could do." She looked at Lake. "That's the way I felt being married. On that swing. Being pushed, with no way to stop it. No . . ." she hesitated searching for the word.

"Control," Lake said it for her and nodded. "It means a great deal. Maybe everything," he said more to himself than Maggie, then he looked at her again. "But caring for a wife, taking care of her is what a husband's supposed to do. Proper."

"Is it, Mr. Mattick?"

He shrugged. "Way it's always been."

She frowned. "That's not a very good answer."

Lake smiled reluctantly. "No," he admitted. "But then, neither is yours."

She smiled too, then shook her head. "I don't know, Mr. Mattick," she said. "It's . . . something I have to do to live with myself. Can you understand that?"

Lake's eyes shadowed slightly. "Yes, ma'am," he nodded. "I can understand that. Maybe better'n you'd expect—"

In the lead, Rufe called, "Let's run'em again."

Lake frowned and glanced at Maggie, realizing he was almost glad he'd talked to her. It had been a long time since he'd—He pushed the feeling back. He had a job to do. Nothing came before that.

"Good luck, Mrs. Calder," he said and strapped his horse out.

"And to you, Mr. Mattick," he heard her say as he pulled away from her.

CHAPTER 8

They ran until Rufe's blue faltered under him again, stumbling and nearly falling. Drawing the horse in, the old scout held up his hand to the others to halt, then looked back at them and, for the first time, felt a kernel of hopelessness twist in his stomach.

They were tired, and the hopelessness was in them too, beginning in their faces, a pale edge in their eyes. All except Lake Mattick. Something was keeping him going, something—

Tim Carmody's horse stumbled, sinking forward, nearly

going down with the red-haired youth and Dick Summers, but Carmody managed to get him back to his feet.

Rufe swung his blue back around, coming in beside Carmody's horse.

"Get on," Rufe ordered the bald-headed man.

"Rufe—"

"I said, get on."

"Maybe one of the others," Dick said.

Rufe shook his head. "You'll ride with me," the old scout said. "This time we ain't discussin' it."

Nodding a weary surrender, the bald-headed man gripped the back of Rufe's saddle, then eased over onto the blue's rump, pain etching his face.

Sitting up, he managed to smile at Rufe. "Keep this up, I'll be able to get a job in a circus." He tried to say it lightly, but his voice was thin and strained.

"You're too damn ugly," Rufe said and nodded down at Dick's foot. "Think it'd be any better in the stirrup?"

"Tried it with Tim. All about the same."

Rufe slipped his foot free.

"Try it a while," he ordered him.

"Who the hell made you the leader?"

"Shut up or I'll bust your other one for you."

Grinning and shaking his head, Dick eased his foot in the wood loop, his breath catching slightly, then he cocked his head. "You know you're always accusin' me of bein' crabby; I think it's you that's gettin' downright fawchey as you get older. Touchy as a teased snake."

"Comes from hangin' around with you."

"Me? Hell, I'm good-natured."

"Yeah, like the time down on the Bayou Salade in Colorado lookin' for salt."

Dick laughed. "That was a helluva set-to wasn't it? Wonder if that Frenchman's still around?"

Rufe shook his head. "Don't think so. Heard he was killed."

"Yeah." Dick nodded. "I recollect I heard that too. Whorehouse someplace."

"Lawdog shot him for ridin' his horse up on the second floor, then takin' one of the girls and—"

Dick laughed. "That was that Frenchman, wasn't it? Damn . . ." he sighed, smiling.

Easing around in the saddle, Rufe looked back over the flat stretch of ground they'd just covered, squinting into the veil of snow.

"Nothin'," the old scout grumbled.

"You sound disappointed."

Rufe looked at him. "Guess I do," he admitted, turning back front in the saddle. "Just like to know where the hell they are. This is like ridin' around blindfolded."

"That'd be a lot safer," Summers commented.

Rufe smiled, then it faded. "Dammit," he growled. "I'd give anything for some decent cover. Goddamn prairie."

"Coulda headed for them mountains."

"Thought about it," Rufe acknowledged. "But New Eden is closer."

"How far you figger?"

Rufe shook his head. "I was only there that one time. Came in from the mountains, then rode south. Never been at it this way. Never had no reason to go back. They weren't real sociable to a nonbeliever. Not far though. To-morrow, early mornin', maybe." His eyes traveled up and around. "Goddamn prairie," he sighed, shaking his head, then nudged the blue into a gentle trot.

———————◄◆►———————

Twilight began to come in the middle of the afternoon. Drifting. White shadow.

It gathered in on the men as they cut through the white, leaving ragged scrawl-like marks. Darkening their features, smoothing them away until they were odd shapes, hulks blended to their horses, further misshapen by jutting rifle barrels.

In the saddle, Rufe Kitrel felt it come, pressing in through his furs as they started up a long steep hill. Slow-ing his blue, he let him walk. No one had said anything in over two hours. Just riding. Running, then walking, run-ning, then walking. And feeling the horses weaken more and more under them, bleeding slowly into the men with the cold.

Angling between the low humps of rocks, Rufe pushed himself up with one hand, and stood in the left stirrup.

The blue rounded a large rock and stepped down.

Suddenly the horse dropped, his hoof slipping on ice-glazed rock, then reeling to one side. Startled, Rufe did two things at once. He lifted the reins and bringing the horse's head up caught the saddle horn with the other hand, keeping himself upright.

Behind him, he heard a surprised bark from Dick Sum-mers and felt the bald-headed man grab his shoulder, then lose it as the horse swung around.

He half saw Dick kicking free of the stirrup, trying to keep from getting hung in it, but in doing it, he completely lost his balance and fell off the horse. He sprawled sidewise, pitching head over heels.

Dick screamed, then slumped motionless into the snow, lying still, letting his breath pound through him.

Reeling his horse back around, Rufe swung to the ground and knelt down beside his friend.

"Dick." Rufe probed.

The bald-headed man trembled and opened his eyes. "Leg's gone now too," he whispered in a tight measured voice.

The others came in beside them and Maggie dismounted, crouching at Dick's leg.

"Mr. Summers," she said, "perhaps I can—"

The bald-headed man shook his head. "No, ma'am, thank you, but there ain't nothin' to be done."

Rufe blinked staring down at Dick, then as if in reflex, he leaned forward shoving his hands under Summers' shoulders and lifted him up.

"Rufe—" Dick protested, but the scout kept pulling him up. "Rufe," the bald-headed man snapped and bringing his arm up, he knocked his friend's hands away.

Stumbling back, Rufe stared at Dick unbelievingly.

"I'm done," the bald-headed man said quietly.

Rufe swallowed. "We're gettin' you to that settlement—"

Summers shook his head. "Rufe," he sighed, "this leg's busted up like rotten wood. I don't think I could get back up on a horse, much less sit one. Even if I could, I'd slow you more. Get us all killed. And I don't particularly want to go to hell with that on my mind." He smiled and shrugged. "Maybe it's time I tried wrestlin' the devil anyway." He looked at Rufe, his eyes softening. "It's my time, old hoss."

Still staring at Dick, Rufe eased back, sitting down in the snow, the acceptance darkening his face. And he nodded.

"Now," Dick said, "how 'bout you boys carryin' me back down there." He pointed to the big rock they had just come around. "Give me somethin' to lean on."

Rufe pulled his eyes up. "Shorty," he called and the small man dismounted, then picked Summers up carefully.

The bald-headed man's breath came hard as they lifted him, then carried him back down to the rock and rested him up against it.

"Mr. Kitrel," Maggie said, "you can't—"

The old man reeled. "Goddammit, Mrs. Calder—" He trembled, then looked to Mattick. "Get her on her horse," he growled.

Stepping down beside her, Mattick took her arm.

Maggie's eyes came around bewildered. "But they can't—"

"We have to," Mattick said coldly. "It's him or us."

Rufe's eyes jerked up. "Get her on that horse," he snapped.

Mattick stared at him, then nodding, he turned back to the animals, and Rufe looked to his friend. Summers was watching Mattick over his shoulder.

Rufe swallowed, stammering. "He don't—"

Summers brought his eyes around. "He's right," the bald-headed man said simply.

"Yeah," Rufe growled, then brought his rifle up. "Leave you this . . ." he began.

Summers shook his head. "Do you more good. That pistol'll do." He pointed to the flintlock, in Rufe's belt. Nodding, Rufe slipped it free and handed it to him.

"Ain't worth a damn," he said. "Gotta be close enough to kick'em in the shin to use it."

Summers nodded. "It'll do."

Rufe squinted back down the hill, then looked to Summers. "You'd better be high-tailin' it," the bald-headed man said.

"Yeah." Rufe swallowed, and turning, walked to his horse and mounted him. He looked at Summers again.

Summers lifted his hand. "Watch your hair," he said.

Rufe tried to smile. "I'd say the same, you bald-headed bastard—" His voice quieted. "Don't kill'em all—" He nodded, then hurriedly swung his horse out, the others following.

They climbed the hill. At the crest Rufe reined his horse in and letting the others go by him, he looked back down the slope.

Dick was sitting against the rock. Like he was lounging on a porch somewhere, feeling the sun.

Rufe started to shout out. To call to him. And frowned. It would do no good. For a moment, he thought about riding back down and staying with him, but that would do no good either. Dick would have it no other way. In his position, neither would he.

"*Companyero*," Rufe whispered, and reeling his horse, spurred him out.

CHAPTER 9

Dick Summers rested back against the rock, peering downslope. He could barely see the bottom of the incline fifty or sixty yards away because of the blending of the snowfall and darkness.

Just as well. He shrugged. If he could see them coming a long way away, he would just get riled. Funny, he mused, this way, he almost felt peaceful.

Shifting the pistol to his left hand, he slipped his Green River knife from its scabbard and held it in his right. Even though he was right-handed, he figured the knife would do him more good than the pistol. He hadn't fired that many pistols and he wasn't too good with one anyhow.

He looked back downslope, trying to concentrate, but found his mind wandering slightly. Oddly enough, he kept thinking about a time nearly twenty years ago when he and Rufe had journeyed to New Orleans. He smiled. All those strange buildings and pretty-talking ladies.

Then after New Orleans on the river barge coming back up the Mississippi, they drank Indian whiskey and spent the whole next day heaving over the side. He could still hear that fat captain laughing.

"What the hell was in that?" Rufe had asked.

"Well that takes some tellin'," the captain grinned. "Get yourself a barrel of water and a couple of gallons of alcohol. Throw in two dabs of strychnine, five bars of soap for head, half a pound of red pepper, three, four bars of tobacco, then sagebrush, and fire it till it's brown."

Rufe swallowed, straining to keep what was left in him down.

"Damn," he sighed tightly. "Wish I hadn't asked."

"Want another round?" The captain laughed, and both Rufe and Dick had gone running to the side again.

Sitting against the rock, Dick sighed a grin. He could still hear that damn captain laughing. That night, he and Rufe had—

Below him something darkened, moving. Bringing Dick's eyes to it. A man. Then another.

Summers' stomach stretched wire-taut as he watched the Indians congeal out of the snowfall at the bottom of the slope. Gaining form as they came. Walking their horses. Weariness sloping their shoulders.

More darkened the white, pushing through the snow-mist. Coming up the incline. Then stopping.

The one in the lead sat motionless, stark against the snowfall. Summers couldn't see his eyes, but he could feel them. Forcing the tightness from him, Summers pushed himself up and forward on his good leg, smiling.

"Hello, boys," he called to them. "What kept you?" he roared, then brought a deep laugh up from his belly.

That would stop them for a moment, he knew, make them think. A man who laughed at death was a warrior.

"Come on," he shouted waving to them, laughing again.

More Indians came out of the snowfall, lining the bottom of the hill.

"Well, lads," he barked, "you figger there are enough of you?" His breath whitened the air, waiting.

"Well—" he shouted. And they exploded toward him like fragments of night. Blinking, he felt a quiver of fear, then it was gone.

He cocked the pistol, turned the sharp edge of the Green River up, and met them.

———————◆———————

Mattick heard something. A voice he thought at first. Muffled. A long way away. Still riding, he turned, listening.

Nothing. The wind stirred in the snow. Then there was

another sound. Sharp and quick. Dulled by snow and distance.

Rufe pulled around. "Shot," he whispered.

Mattick nodded. "About fifteen minutes back," he gauged matter-of-factly.

Rufe's eyes came around. "Yeah," he replied tautly. "About fifteen minutes back. He's buyin' us a little time." He glared at Mattick. "They taught you real good in that war didn't they?" he growled and spurred his horse out.

Mattick watched him, then nodded quietly. "Yeah," he whispered. "Real good."

CHAPTER 10

Night pressed in on them, weaving through the snow. Mattick stretched in the saddle and watched the woman riding ahead of him.

She was doing a lot better than he would have expected, but it was catching up with her now. She wavered slightly in the saddle, then steadied herself on the saddle horn.

"Hang on," Mattick whispered to himself.

He had been in the saddle and on the move as much as three days at a time, and he always wondered when he had to do it again, how he'd done it before. In the lead, Rufe raised his hand, then motioned to dismount.

"Gotta rest these animals," he said. "'Sides"—he frowned gazing upward—"in five more minutes we'll have trouble seeing the ground. Mrs. Calder"—he looked at her —"you stay in the saddle. Rest of you get down and take the horse's tail in front of you. Mrs. Calder, you ride in front and I'll direct you."

"I'll walk too," Maggie said.

"Mrs. Calder," Rufe sighed patiently, "just do as I tell you."

"I've been doing as I've been told too long—"

"Goddammit," Rufe snapped, then frowned. "Scuse me, ma'am, but this ain't no time to be provin' somethin'. Now do what I tell you. You may have to do some walkin' later."

"How far we gonna hoof it?" Carmody asked.

"Further'n you'll want," Rufe assured him. "All right," he said to Maggie, gesturing for her to move out. She frowned and nudged her horse out, grudgingly. Rufe followed her, taking her horse's tail. Rufe's horse came by, and Mattick grasped the coarse hair.

"Hope none of these animals are spooked," Carmody grumbled.

"Or ate much lately," Shorty added.

Lake felt the wince of a smile in his stiff lips, then Rufe's horse pulled him out. Walking, Lake began to realize how tired he was. The snow was just below his knees and he followed in the wake of Rufe and his horse.

In front of the blue, Lake could see the old man striding out without missing a step, and in front of him, the woman.

They slogged up and over a small hogback. Through small brush and sharp rocks, then down again.

Lake had to concentrate to keep moving. The more he walked, the more he thought about how tired he was and lifting his feet began to take effort. He had to tell them to move, and the more he did that, the more he could feel his strength whispering from him, the monotony, the sameness, and the cold dragging him down. His hands and feet were already numb.

"Jesus," he murmured.

Rufe glanced back. "What?"

Lake shook his head. "Nothin'," he answered.

Rufe's old eyes nearly softened. "You were in the cavalry too long. Take'em one at a time," the old man said. "Don't think about the long run." Turning, he pushed on.

Sparse aspen shadowed around them like drifting shafts of night. The snow was shallower in the trees, and the going a little easier. Lake counted the aspen. Then the trees were gone, and they pushed out into a flat.

Marching again, Lake thought and shook his head. Wandering that circle in time. He dragged his eyes up trying to see, but the light was gone. Everything had blended into itself, wrapping darkness around them.

He pushed on, doing like Rufe said. Concentrating on the walk, not on where they were going or what was ahead or behind. Just the walking. Just the moving.

They topped a shallow rise, then started down along the slope of a hill. Sudden branches caught Lake in the

face, raking across his cheek, breaking ice crystals that
had formed in the beginnings of his beard, leaving a
swath of pain.

Jerking, the ex-soldier blinked, the throbbing in his
cheek the only thing he could feel. The rest of him was
numb. Formless.

"Jesus," he whispered-thought and pushed on through
more branches, into a scattering of brush and low piñon
that became a labyrinth in the darkness. Bulling into
them, Lake rounded a small hill and started up again,
when he heard something behind him.

It was a scream, followed by the breaking of wood, and
the hummph of something ramming into the snow.

"Rufe," he tried to shout, but it came a moan. Concentrating, he put strength into his voice. "Rufe—"

Ahead, the blue roan slowed, then stopped. A form
slogged around the horse.

"What is it?"

"Somebody's down," Lake answered. They staggered,
meeting Shorty as they went.

"It's Carmody's horse," the little man said, pointing
through the crisscross of limbs and darkness. "Tim went
after him." Below, about ten feet down, Lake was able to
make out two figures in the snow.

Rufe nodded and looked at Maggie. "Stay here a minute, ma'am," he said, then turned angling down the slope
toward the man and horse.

"Stay with the woman," Mattick said to Shorty and followed Rufe.

Stumbling through an outcropping of rock, they sank
up to their thighs in a snowbank. Rufe went on as if it

wasn't there, and he and Lake pushed through it to Carmody and his mare. The horse was down, resting on her knees, and Carmody was pulling at her reins trying to get her back up.

The red-haired youngster looked around as the two men approached, and shook his head.

"Sorry, Rufe," he said, "but she stepped down into deep snow and couldn't seem to get back up. Then she went over." The old man nodded and squinted down at the animal.

"Tired." He frowned. "Just damn well worn out. If we don't get her up, she'll die right there."

Walking to the horse, the old man knelt down in front of her, and put out his hand touching her nose. The horse's head bobbed up slightly. The old man eased down closer to her, taking her head in his hands, lifting her nose up to his, then touching noses, he breathed into her nostrils. The horse's ears rotated front and back, and after a moment, Rufe stood up, and grasping her bridle, he walked in a half circle around to the back, bringing her head around. Moving, he slipped his fur cap off his head and held it down in front of her.

Seeing the cap, the mare twisted to reach it, but couldn't make it. Her legs came under her gradually, then awkwardly she pushed up, staggering to her feet to get to the cap.

"Damn," Carmody sighed with relief, "I thought she was done for."

Rufe shook his head. "No more'n the others. None of 'em got much left in 'em. They all need feed." He frowned and, squinting into the darkness and snowfall, he slipped his cap back on and raked his foot across the ground, then leaned down brushing the snow aside, uncovering wads of new blue stem.

"Some grass here." He nodded. "Not much but it'll do," he said, standing up, then looked up the hill. "Shorty," he called.

"Yeah?"

"You and Mrs. Calder come on down," he said, "and bring the blue and the Morgan."

"How come?"

"Just do it," Rufe snapped and looked back at Carmody. "Knock some of this snow aside," he told him, "and let her feed." He turned to Lake. "Best get at it."

"Rufe," Lake began to protest, "the Absoraka could—"

"I know"—the old man nodded—"but the next horse that goes down might not get up."

Frowning, Lake nodded his agreement and started raking snow with his boot. Maggie and Shorty came down the hill and dismounted. Shorty saw Lake and Carmody kicking the snow around and looked to Rufe.

"What the hell are—?"

"Lettin' the horses feed," the old man answered. "And while they're doin' it," he said, turning to the others, "unload 'em. Throw ever'thin' off but saddles and ammunition."

As the horses craned their heads down to the grass, Rufe untied his bedroll and let it drop. Pulling his saddlebags off, he removed a package from them, then tossed them aside too. Unwrapping the package, he walked to Maggie and handed her one of the cakes inside.

"What is it?" she asked.

"Pemmican," he answered. Her eyes narrowed questioningly.

"Venison." Rufe smiled. "Dried, mixed with tallow and blackberries."

Maggie bit into it hesitantly, chewed slowly, then took another bite. "You know"—she swallowed—"that's good."

"Yes'um," Rufe nodded, and after giving a cake to the others, he wrapped the package and slipped it in his coat pocket.

He was walking back to his horse, when Lake stopped him. "Back there—"

"Yeah?"

"When you put your nose against the mare's, what were you doin'?"

The old man took a bite of pemmican. "Seen the Indians do it. Tie a horse down, then breathe in his nostrils. Part of breakin'em. Calms'em . . . makes friends with'em . . . somethin' like that. You ever notice that's the way horses greet each other? Seen many a spooky horse calmed that way." He walked on to the blue and picked up his reins. "Anyway"—he shrugged, pushing the last of the pemmican in his mouth—"sometimes it works. Sometimes it don't. Most of the time it does."

He looked to the others. "Supper's over," he said and pointed around the hill. "Mrs. Calder." He nodded.

Maggie mounted up and nudged her horse out. Rufe took the tail of her horse as she came by him, then followed. Mattick fell in next, then Shorty and Carmody.

Maggie led them around the base of the hill, and Rufe directed her between two more ghosted slopes, when he heard the sound of water.

"Mrs. Calder," he called and she pulled in, and the old man hesitated, trying to pick out the direction.

"Rufe?" Lake asked.

"Stream," the old man replied. "Down the end of these slopes." He nodded. "Butt those saddles."

They mounted up and Rufe took the lead, pushing down the hills to the stream. He reined up on the bank and let the blue drink as he surveyed the stream. There wasn't much water, but it would cover their tracks.

Rufe waited until all the horses had drunk, then he pushed the blue over the bank and turned downstream.

"Last time we tried this—" Shorty began.

"Last time ain't this time," Rufe said. "Damn, Shorty," he sighed, "can't you ever see the bright side of things?"

It was silent for a moment, then Shorty cleared his throat. "Well," he said, "reckon if we get killed, we'll keep pretty good."

Rufe laughed aloud. "There you go."

They rode for what Rufe gauged to be about a mile, then Rufe angled out of the water onto the opposite bank, through a bed of gravel and dismounted. Stretching, he looked up and around. The snow was beginning to ebb back a little.

"Lettin' up," he said, and watched Lake, Shorty, and Carmody stand down. Maggie came around front. Rufe was turning to catch her horse's tail and saw the glimmer of metal on Lake's saddle. It was his saber.

"Might as well throw that off too," the old man pointed. Lake looked at the saber, then the old man.

"It stays," he stated flatly.

"Ain't worth the—"

"It stays," Lake said again, his voice hardening.

The old man frowned. "It stays," he agreed. "Mrs. Calder—" he said to the woman, and grasped her horse's tail.

They cut away from the stream and started up a low ridge. Climbing, Rufe felt the air stir around him, and as he topped the rise, the snowfall rushed around him, thinning. Then it was gone.

Stars rustled in the black sky, and the moon was stark white, washing the land in a pale glowing light, outlining small hills, mesas, and the mountains off to the west.

Rufe trembled slightly. Another country, he thought. Like somethin' somebody would dream. He glanced back. The sky and land ended in a dark mist.

"Storm's between us and them," he said. "We can make time now." Stumbling back to the blue, he mounted him.

"Short walk," Carmody said, lifting himself into the saddle.

Shorty and Lake pulled themselves up silently, and Rufe turned his horse down the ridge, walking the animal as he scanned the ground. It was fairly level, easy sloping ground. He looked back at the horses, then at the slope again.

"Carmody," he called.

"Yessir?"

"How's that horse steppin'?"

"Well as ever, I reckon."

Rufe nodded and glanced at Lake. Lake knew what he was thinking.

"Might make the difference," the ex-soldier said.

"Yeah," Rufe growled, "or kill a horse." He pondered it a second more and nodded. It was too good a chance to pass up. "'Least they been watered and fed. A little."

He looked at Maggie. "Hold on," he said, then strapped his horse out, pushing him down the hill, stretching him to a run.

He had never run a horse at night, except over ground he knew, and then he didn't make a practice of it. It was a stupid thing to do, a desperate one, but he almost enjoyed the movement of the horse and the wind in his face.

Suddenly they were all in a run, blasting through the snow together, pulling astride of each other, then holding the horses in, the hammering of the animals' breathing and hooves mixing.

Next to Lake, Maggie's horse pulled his feet up and was airborne for a second, jumping a small branch. He felt a snap of panic, then saw her balance herself with the stirrups, leaning into the horse, taking the shock as he hit the ground again running.

Down the line, Carmody laughed, and they were out on the flat, clamoring through the sage, threading the snow-covered humps. They ran the flat, then Rufe began to draw them in again as they approached a hill. Turning his horse back to the woman, he nodded at her.

"Mighty well done, ma'am," he said.

Maggie laughed. "Thank you, Mr. Kitrel."

Mattick reined his horse in, then Shorty and Carmody brought theirs up, the grins still on their faces.

"Good ridin', Mrs. Calder," Carmody said. She nodded again.

Shorty shook his head, sighing. "Most as much fun as a fandango with easy ladies—" He glanced at Maggie. "Scuse me, ma'am."

Maggie smiled. "I'm sure it was," she said.

"If we could just talk the Absoraka into comin', it'd be a helluva time," Rufe said.

Shorty's eyes jerked around, staring at the old man. Rufe's lips parted in a smile, and he slapped Shorty on the shoulder.

"Ain't that right, Pork eater?"

Blinking, Shorty's mouth eased into a reluctant smile, then he laughed too. "I reckon," he said.

Young Carmody joined them, but Lake glanced back up the ridge. "We're wastin' time," he said.

The laughter eased away. "Yeah," Rufe agreed and nudged his horse out through the sage. The others followed, the laughter gone now.

The ghost of a smile lingered on old Rufe's face. For a minute there it had been like the old times. The boys rendezvousing . . . and the smile drifted . . . those times were gone . . . like Dick . . . like him soon. His eyes slipped to Lake Mattick.

"Ain't much of a joiner, are you?" he said, feeling an edge of sudden anger as he said it.

The ex-soldier's eyes met his.

"No." He finally shook his head. "Closer you get to people, the harder it is to watch'em die," he said. Then nudging his horse, he moved out and away.

Rufe watched him and the anger ebbed back a little. There was something about Mattick that echoed in himself.

"Hell," he growled, and strapped his horse out.

They moved up the hill, then down a folding of broken slopes, keeping off the skylines.

Beneath him, Rufe felt his horse tiring again. Might not should've run, he thought, but it had done his mind good, and they might have gained a little on the Absorakas.

"Mrs. Calder," he called and reined his horse in. Maggie slowed to a halt, and Rufe, Lake, Shorty, and Camody dismounted. Rufe smiled at her and nodded.

"The lead's yours," he said.

Returning the smile, she nodded, nudging her horse out, and riding, she felt the smile for a long time. Odd, she thought. She had never felt as if she was a real part of anything before. Everything else had come because she was either a woman or a wife.

When she and John had come to the post five years ago, she had been accepted into the circle of women only because she was a woman, and because she was a woman, she had joined them because it was the thing to do.

She glanced back at the men. Earlier all she had been able to feel was fear. A little of that was gone now because of what she felt for these men. A link of some sort. Something she'd earned.

And it helped.

———————◆———————

They walked for another hour, twisting their way through the hills, then came into the open again, onto what seemed to be a long vast plain.

Ahead, Lake heard Rufe tell Maggie to stop and they

both pulled up. Stretching, Rufe squinted into the bright moonlight, examining the ground.

The sky and ground were clear, sweeping into each other, flat as far as Lake could see except for what looked like low craggy hills a long way off. He started around Rufe's horse when suddenly the old man wheeled, swinging up into his saddle and running across the flat ground.

"What the hell's he doin'?" Shorty asked.

Turning, Lake swung up into his saddle, and went after the old man. As he went by Maggie, she strapped her horse out, joining him.

They followed Rufe about half a mile, when the old man reeled his horse in, bringing him up short, and looked down. Lake was almost to the old man when he saw it too.

"Pull him in," he shouted to Maggie, and they both jerked their horses in, skidding through the snow. Patting his Morgan, calming him, Lake eased him alongside Rufe's blue.

"Jesus," he whispered, looking down. They were on a cliff.

CHAPTER 11

Dismounting, Mattick walked out to the edge and knelt down. Tim and Shorty rode in behind them.

"What the hell, we—" Shorty began, then swallowed. "Damn," he murmured.

Beneath Lake the slope dropped away sharply at about a fifty-degree angle into a valley six or seven hundred yards below. Rufe came up next to him, and stood staring down the slope.

"If it ain't one thing, it's another," he sighed.

"See a trail?" Carmody asked, dismounting.

"If there is one, snow's got it covered," Rufe answered curtly.

"Maybe if we ride on a bit," Shorty put in, still on his horse.

Rufe glanced up and down the edge, then shook his head. "Don't think so. We could ride all night trying to find another way."

"We can crisscross it," Mattick said, standing. "Go down at a long angle across it, then double back. Take a while, but it's the only way we're gonna get down from here."

"Wait a minute," Shorty snapped. "You mean we're goin' down here?"

"I am," Lake nodded, turning back to his horse.

"What if the rest of us got a mind to do it another way?"

"Then I'll go it alone."

"Goddammit," Rufe cut in. "Ain't nobody goin' it alone." He looked up at the little man. "Shorty, we're goin' down that slope, so get down from there and let's get at it."

"Just don't like him and his ways sometimes," Shorty grumbled.

"I don't either," Rufe allowed. "But he's right." He looked up at Maggie as Shorty stood down. "Looks like you're gonna get to walk after all," he said to her as she lowered herself to the ground. "Think you'll be all right?"

Maggie's eyes came up, narrowing. "Mr. Kitrel—"

"Yes'm—"

"Stop asking me that. Every time you do it reminds me

how frightened I am. I've got no choice anyway. Just go ahead."

The old man's eyes softened. "Yes'm," he acknowledged, then glanced at the others. "Stay in single file," he instructed them, "like we have been, and whatever you do stay in the tracks that have been made."

Reaching up he slipped his rifle from its boot, then turned to the edge.

"Want me to take it?" Mattick asked.

Rifle shook his head. "My job," he said, and his eyes dropped to the slope. "Goddamn prairie," he sighed, then gripping his rifle by the barrel he eased over the side, probing in front with the stock. Sinking into the snow, he tested his footing.

"Dirt and gravel, mostly," he said back over his shoulder.

Mattick dropped over the side. Then Maggie, Shorty, and Carmody.

Squinting down the slope, Rufe's eyes scanned folds and drops, and he felt his stomach tightening. Now that they were on the incline, it seemed a damn sight steeper. He looked down and a swallow rippled through his throat. It was a long way to the bottom.

Lifting the butt, he pushed into the snow. Found dirt. And moved on. A house-sized rock rose up in front of them. Rufe tucked in close to it, found good footing, and they skirted it quickly, down through a clump of sage and out onto a shelf of rock.

Rufe hesitated. The shelf widened, rising up and away from the incline. There would be no way off, he nodded, and turned back through the sage, dropping down the side of the shelf.

The snow deepened between the giant rock and the shelf. Rufe pushed his rifle in and it sank all the way to his hand.

"Damn." He frowned and stepped into it. He dropped into snow up to his waist. Pushing against it, he had a sudden picture in his mind of Shorty going in over his head and wandering around lost like that until it thawed.

A grin broke across his face, and he started to call back to the little man, but then thought better of it. Instead, he pulled his horse alongside him, and let him shove through to the bottom of the shelf, into shallower snow. Then the old man waded out front and led the horse again.

Keeping in close to where the shelf jutted out of the slope, Rufe followed it until it eased away, blending back into the rocks. He angled down again, and the incline began to steepen.

Rufe edged along the face, using his rifle for support. Behind him his horse slipped his footing, stumbling to his knees. Rufe stopped. The blue jacked his knees under him and raised up.

"Good fella," the old man whispered gently, and glanced back to the top.

Nothing yet. Turning, he looked down. They weren't even halfway.

"Damn," he sighed to himself, then stepped out.

The slope lifted beneath him gradually, then he came down on the beginnings of a waist-high sandstone outcropping. Keeping above it, Rufe crossed above a draw between the outcropping and a giant boulder. The old man peered down the channel. The snow in it was shallow but the incline was steep as hell. He considered it a moment, then shook his head, and pushed on over the boulder hoping there might be some better way down. Crossing the crown of the rock, he eased down the far side.

The ground steepened sharply under the old man. Moving slowly, he leaned against the boulder, and probed the snow with his rifle, dropping it forward, then pushing it down until he had sunk it up to the tip of the barrel.

Frowning, he covered the end of the barrel with his hand, and eased the Hawken on down. He stopped when the snow touched his forearm. Still no solid ground.

"Damn prairie," he growled and dragged the Hawken out of the snow.

"We gotta go back," he said and turned up the slope.

The others climbed back to the crown of the boulder and Rufe followed them. Topping the rock, he started across it, then stopped, his eyes jerking to the crest. No movement.

"What is it?" Mattick asked.

The old man shook his head slowly. "Thought I heard somethin'—"

Mattick's eyes followed Rufe's. "I don't see anything," he said, easing his gaze down. "Let's go—"

Shrugging, the old mountain man nodded. "Yeah," he agreed, turning. "We—"

He caught the flicker of something out of the corner of his eye, but he never really heard the arrow in flight.

None of them did.

Only the thump as it rammed through Tim Carmody's back, pitching him forward into his horse. Startled, the horse reared, spinning Carmody into the rock and snow.

Twisting, Rufe looked back to the rim. He could see them now. Shadows stark against the sky. Another arrow slammed into the saddle beside Mattick's head, a shot split the air, then there were arrows all over the place, filling the air.

"Down there," Rufe shouted, pointing to the draw between the boulder and the sandstone outcropping.

Next to Rufe, Shorty turned, scrambling back toward Carmody.

"Shorty," the old man barked, but it did no good. The little man kept running.

"Get her out of here," Rufe yelled to Mattick, then shoving the blue's reins into Mattick's hand, the old man pushed by him, running toward Shorty and Carmody.

Reeling, Mattick shouted to Maggie, and she followed him across the boulder, then down the incline between the boulder and the sandstone.

Arrows rattled down around Rufe and Shorty, but Shorty kept going, letting go of his horse's reins, diving the last few feet to his friend, nearly landing on top of him.

"Tim," he screamed, gripping the young man's shoulder, jerking him over. "Tim—"

The old man rushed in behind Shorty, and burying his hands in the little man's coat, he hauled him back and up.

"Tim—" the little man sobbed.

"He's dead," Rufe growled, and nearly lifting Shorty off

the ground, Rufe turned him back down the rock. "Now get out of here—"

Bewildered, Shorty stopped completely, looking up at the old man.

"Goddammit," the old man raged. "Get the hell out of here—" Nodding, Shorty blinked and reeled, picking up his horse's reins, and ran down the rock.

Catching up Carmody's horse, Rufe fell in behind Shorty's animal and, below them, the old man could see Mattick and the woman. They were rounding the base of the giant rock. Making it to cover.

Shorty started down the slope and, slipping, hit on his butt, then pushed out, running, dragging his horse down behind him.

"Take it easy," Rufe shouted, but the little man and his horse were already moving too fast, careening down the draw, sliding over the ice and rock. Then Shorty's horse screamed, his front feet sinking under him, his head pitching down.

"Shorty," the old man shouted.

Reeling, the little man saw his horse falling and, still turning, he threw himself into the side of the boulder. His horse plunged down the slope, plowing through the snow and dirt, tumbling end over end into the bright darkness.

Still running, Rufe tried to keep himself in check, but it was nearly impossible. For a moment, he thought he might lose Carmody's horse too, but he dug his moccasins into the snow and gravel, slowing himself a little.

"Come on," he barked at Shorty as he charged by him. Nodding, the little man followed and the two of them hurdled down the draw. The rifle crashed above them, sending a ball raking across the boulder.

A few yards from the base, Rufe hugged the side of the huge rock and, slipping on a patch of ice, he planted his heels in the snow and vaulted forward, diving the last few feet to cover.

Vaguely stunned, he felt the horse go around him, then somebody took it. Mattick. The old man nodded and was shoving a hand under himself to get up when Shorty slammed across his legs.

The two men lay there a moment, then Lake pulled the old man up behind the boulder. He turned to Shorty, but the little man shook his head.

"I can do it," he wheezed.

Nodding, Lake turned up the slope past the woman sitting on the ground next to the horses. Rufe nodded to her. Breathless, she nodded back to him.

"I won't ask," he said. She smiled weakly.

Beyond her, Lake jerked his Henry from its boot and slipped back along the base of the boulder to where they'd come down and edged a look back up at the crest.

"Jesus," Shorty gasped. "You see that horse?"

Rufe nodded. "Easy place to lose one. One wrong step'll do it."

"Jesus," Shorty sighed resting back against the boulder, closing his eyes.

"Damn prairie," Rufe swallowed and, wiping the snow out of his face, the old man glanced toward the horses, then down, surveying their position. A deep frown thinned his lips.

The boulder was their only cover. On the side they

came down, there was the sandstone outcropping, but it ended twenty feet above them. On the far side, there was just a scattering of rocks.

Below them, the slope dropped away steeply. He looked it over several times before he saw the gathering of sage and stunted piñon pines, about sixty yards down. It was the only break in the slope. Leastways the only one he could see.

His eyes eased down. The next cover was a shelf, another hundred yards beyond the sage and piñons. From the shelf it was only a few yards to the bottom and out onto the flat ground.

He considered it a moment. Two hundred yards to the shelf, he gauged and looked up. The boulder would cover them part of the way to the piñons, but they would be in the open a little better than a hundred and fifty yards.

Shaking his head, he eased back against the boulder. Not the best of odds, he frowned. Not the best at all.

But it was all they had.

CHAPTER 12

The scrape of gravel tugged Rufe's eyes up. Lake was pushing down the base of the boulder toward him.

The old man sat forward. "They on their way?"

Lake shook his head and crouched beside Rufe and Shorty. "Looks like they're waitin' on us. They got us by the short hair and they know it."

Rufe nodded. "Yeah," he sighed. "They have at that." It was silent for a moment. The wind moved over the rocks.

Shorty looked up at the old man. "What do you figger, Rufe?"

The old man shook his head. "I don't know." He frowned and looked at the sky. "Got about two hours till daylight. Might as well take it easy for a bit. Go down to the turn there and keep an eye out. And here—" He reached into his coat pocket and pulled out the package of pemmican. "Have a chew."

"Thanks." Shorty nodded taking it, then moved out.

Rufe handed cakes to Lake and Maggie and they ate in silence, almost wolfing down the food. When they had finished, Rufe got his canteen from his horse, took it to Shorty, let him drink, then returned to Lake and Maggie. Rufe sat down and passed the canteen, and the two men looked down the slope.

Lake eased forward. "To the piñons, then the shelf, you think?"

Rufe looked up. He nodded. "You got a good eye, boy."

"About a hundred-twenty yards in the open."

"Closer to one-fifty. Little better."

"Yeah." The ex-soldier frowned. "Question is, how to get from here to there." He glanced back up. "Only good thing is, maybe this damn cliff will stop the Indians. Then we could just head on to Cunningham's."

"They'll come down it," Rufe assured him. "And they'll come down it hard." The old man took another sip of water, staring at the young man for a long moment. "And there you go about Cunningham's again—"

Lake blinked, then pulled his eyes away. "Just . . . figurin'." He shrugged and looked down the slope, trying to change the subject. "Think I'll—"

"Who is he?" Rufe cut in.

Lake's eyes jerked around. "What?"

"The man at Cunningham's," Rufe said. "The one you're after."

Rufe could see Lake's hand tremble slightly and he shook his head. "Don't know what you're talkin' about."

Rufe shook his head. "I been a hunter too long, not to know the smell of another one. 'Sides you want to get to Cunningham's too bad. When I asked you about it back at camp, you lied. And when it's somethin' a man'll lie about, it's usually killin' he has in mind."

Lake stood up. "None of your concern," he said and started to turn toward the horses, but Rufe stood up blocking his way.

Rufe nodded. "Ordinarily I'd agree with you. But your wantin' to get to Cunningham's is liable to get in the way of your thinkin' straight, and get us all killed. That makes it my concern. Now who is he?"

"Rufe—" Lake whispered, his hand tightening on the grip of the Henry. Behind Rufe, Maggie stood up slowly.

"Mr. Mattick," she said quietly.

A muscle spasmed in Lake's jaw, and blinking, he glanced at Maggie, then lowered the rifle. "His name is Quincy," Lake said, his voice tightening. "Major James Quincy. He killed fifty-seven men."

"My God," Maggie gasped. "Fifty-seven. How could anybody—?"

Lake shook his head. "He didn't do it personally. Not with his hands. But by giving an order." He swallowed. "An order that was wrong. And fifty-seven men died. One of them . . ." He trembled. "One of them was a friend of mine," he said and pushed by Rufe. "Now if you don't mind, I'm gonna see about getting down from here."

"Mr. Mattick," he heard Maggie say behind him, but he kept walking. Around the horses, then down along the base of the rock twenty feet until he came to where the boulder rounded into the ground, and there was nothing but open slope in front of him.

Crouching down, he pressed his back against the rock and stared down the slope, not really seeing what was there.

Trembling, he closed his eyes, and felt time rustling in him. Time and dead men. All there at once. Blended, joined like dark gemini.

His eyes snapped open, and he forced calm through himself. He had to get hold. And he had to get off this goddamn slope.

Pushing everything else from his mind, he eased forward and squinted down into the bright darkness. Below him, the slope fell away steeply. Barren. Only rocks and snow. Frowning, he looked up. It was the same.

Leaning back against the rock, he thought for a moment, then stood up and looked at the sandstone outcropping at the top of the boulder, then moved his gaze down the slope to the piñons and the shelf beyond it. He nodded. There was only one way to do it.

"Damn," he growled, and picked up his rifle, then made his way back to the horses and past them. Rufe still was with Maggie. They were finishing their pemmican.

"Find anything?" Rufe asked.

Lake shook his head. "There's no way out of here but straight down from here to those trees, then the shelf. But I think I've figured a way."

"How?"

"I'm going to lay back in that sandstone and put down cover for you. With the Henry, I can do it."

"Why you?"

"Because it's my rifle."

The old man shook his head. "I don't like it."

"Neither do I, but it's all we got."

"I can't let you do that for us—"

"I'm not," Lake cut him off.

The old man's eyes came up staring at him. "You sure got a one track mine, ain't you, son."

"Yeah." Lake nodded. "Now let's get to it."

CHAPTER 13

Lake loaded the Henry while Shorty, Rufe, and Maggie went for the horses. Finishing with the rifle, he checked the cartridge box, making sure the catch was secure, and pulled his gloves on tight. As the others came back toward him, he stood up.

"I'm going back to the top of the draw. Into that sandstone. When I get there move out. And move fast. I've got sixteen shots, and that should get you to those piñons. Stop there and I'll have to reload. That's gonna be the one snag. Like I've said before, this thing is hell to load. It may take a little time. But wait for me to start shooting again. Then move to the shelf, and then the bottom. Then you cover me. I oughta be able to get down faster without a horse."

Rufe nodded. "With daylight coming we can run the horses the rest of the way to the settlement. Most of those Absoraka still on the bluff, we might just make it." Nodding, Lake edged to the side of the boulder.

"Mattick," Shorty said stopping him, and Lake looked back. Shorty cleared his throat with difficulty. "Thanks," he said. Lake stared at him for a moment. Then wordlessly he turned bursting into the open.

Charging up the draw, Lake kept low, running at a crouch. Then hitting the sharp upslope, he slammed to his knees, squinting into the silver darkness, trying to pick movement off the rim.

Seeing nothing, he pushed himself up and began crawling up the rock, back through the trail they had cut on the way down, then into new snow, trying to keep as close to the boulder as possible.

He stopped halfway up, easing his raw breath through him, his eyes searching the folds and creases of the incline. A thin wind brushed across him, chilling the sweat that was beginning to gather on his face. Below him a horse snorted.

Swallowing, he shoved himself up again, crawl-running through the snow. Nearing the top of the boulder, he angled across the draw, and into the outcropping of sandstone, and sank into it.

Weaving through the rock, staying low Lake made his

way to the top of the outcropping, then found a niche between two humps of sandstone, and dropping to his knees he stretched out slowly.

Bringing the rifle up, his eyes caught the outline of a form on the top of the boulder. He swung the Henry around, then realized it was Carmody's body.

The wind had rustled snow over it, so that the dead man seemed to be blending slowly into the rock, one knee raised partially, and his arm twisted up over his head so that it looked as if he was waving at Mattick to come with him. To follow.

A colorless echo calling . . . Trembling, Lake dragged his eyes away from the dead man.

"Foolish," he said aloud and looked up the slope. The wind laced across him. White silence pressed in around him, and he could feel Carmody out there.

"Rufe," he growled, but kept his eyes on the crest line. "Come on—"

Then down the draw, he heard the scrape of horses' hooves. Almost thankful, he raised the rifle.

Seeing Lake go into the rocks, Rufe began a long ten count.

"Rufe . . ." Shorty whispered anxiously. The old man nodded but kept counting; then finishing, he moved.

Bolting upright, he plunged down the steep slope, rifle in one hand, leading the blue and Mattick's Morgan with his other hand. Running.

His feet rammed through snow and gravel, the snow keeping the loose rocks from rolling, but it seemed awfully loud anyway. As if he were falling through dry aspen limbs. He glanced back. Maggie was with him. Then Shorty.

Leaping over a small rock, catching another with his foot, the old man swung back, turning and angling straight for the clump of piñons. He could feel the boulder leaving them and the openness yawning around him.

"Damn prairie . . ." he half-muttered and plummeted downward. Running, the old man tried to keep himself in check, but he was moving faster and faster, gaining momentum as he shot down the slope. Behind him, he heard one of the horses stumble, but he kept going. Below him, he could see the piñons. Thirty more yards, he thought—

And the shot split the air above him.

<hr>

Lying on the sandstone, Lake only caught a fragment of movement on the rim, then heard the shot crash down the slope.

That son-of-a-bitch with the rifle. Rising up, he fired out of reflex.

Suddenly the rim rippled alive with moving shadows and pieces of shadows. Lake levered two shots up at them.

"Three," he counted his shots.

The whine of arrows split the air around him and shafts of wood rattled over the sandstone. A figure came over the side. Lake put the barrel on him, following him for a breadth's length, then he fired, knocking the Indian flat in the snow.

"Four."

A second shot crashed from the rim, blasting the sand-stone beside his head, driving him down. Three men burst over the top of the bluff.

Rising up, Lake held his breath and took his time. He dropped the first brave and, levering the Henry, he moved to the second, squeezing the shot off just as the barrel found him.

The third brave leapt over the second, twisting into the snow and Lake caught him in mid-air.

"Seven." He had nine shots left.

Another shot ripped across the sandstone in front of him, and firing without a target, Lake pumped four shots up the slope.

The air around him was sliced by a sudden shock of arrows, but below him, he could see Rufe, Shorty, and Maggie.

They had made it to the clump of piñons.

More arrows rattled down around him, and a shot bit a chunk of rock out over his head.

"Time to move," the ex-soldier whispered and pushing himself down, he dropped into the twisting sandstone.

———————◆———————

In the piñons, Rufe swung the horses to cover. He waited until Maggie and Shorty made it to cover, then handing the woman the reins to both horses, he and Shorty scurried back up to the base of a tree. Crouching down, Rufe lifted his rifle and squeezed a shot off. Next to him Shorty waited until Rufe began reloading, then fired.

An arrow thumped into the ground in front of the old man, then another split the wood above his head.

"That son-of-a-bitch with the long gun ain't bad," the old man grumbled, raising his Hawken and firing back.

"Like to get him," Shorty growled, easing up and squeezing off his shot.

Rufe finished reloading his rifle and fired as a rush of arrows swept through the small trees. Twisting, the old man ducked, pulling his head in.

"Dammit, Mattick," he whispered. "Get that thing loaded."

———◆———

Lake slipped a cartridge into the chamber of the Henry and closing it, eased up over a chest-high rock and pumped off four quick shots.

Another shot bit into the rocks after him, and rising up, Lake levered off five shots, scattering them over the top of the bluff, then ducked down and began crawling for a new position. Below him, he could hear the sound of running. Rufe, Shorty, and Maggie were moving.

Keeping the Henry out of the snow, he wound his way through the morass of sandstone. Above him, the man with the rifle fired at the three downslope.

"Damn him," Lake growled and pumped off two wild shots.

A swatch of arrows raked the air over his head forcing him back into the rocks. Crouching, Lake's eyes combed the outcropping for a better spot. He had to get that bastard with— The Indian's long gun crashed in the darkness again.

"Goddamn him—" Lake breathed and was levering the rifle when he heard the horse scream down the slope.

———◆———

Plunging over a low line of rocks, Rufe heard the shot, then the horse's agonized shriek. The old man twisted around. He could only half see the little man behind Maggie and her horse. He could make out that the horse Shorty was leading had been hit in the rump and his hind leg was going out from under him.

Falling.

For a second, Rufe thought Shorty was trying to hold him. Gripping the reins with his right hand, balancing himself with his rifle in the other, trying to hold the horse up.

"Shorty," the old man yelled. "Let—"

Then he saw Shorty's hand. It was wrapped in the leather. He must have done it on the way down to keep from losing the animal.

The horse struggled mindlessly to regain his feet. He put weight on his wounded leg and it gave under him. Reeling in panic, the animal fought the imprisoning reins Shorty held, jerking his head back, hauling the man with him as his legs gave under him, and he began to roll backward down the hill.

Before Rufe could do anything, they were both plummeting away from him. The little man snapped like a fish on the line. Never screaming.

Just silently gone.

The old man stared at them crashing down the slope. Then a shot jerked his head up. And turning he ran.

———————◄◆►————————

In the rocks, Lake saw Shorty fall, then reeled firing once and ran upward, over the tops of the boulders, and leapt into a sink at the high end of the sandstone.

Levering the Henry, he crawled up the rampart of rocks and slipped the barrel up over them. Squeezing off a shot, he hesitated, eyes poised, waiting for the rifle flash.

Arrows slashed down the slope, but he made himself hold off firing. He wanted the man with the rifle.

His finger sweated on the trigger and he thought his bladder was going to rip open. Then he saw it. A quick spear of flame to his left. Twisting up, he fired in reflex, putting a slug square at it.

He only half heard the roll of the two shots echoing into each other when the rock exploded in front of him blasting his face and eyes with needles of sand.

Screaming, he reeled back, stumbling, and dropping the Henry; he toppled backward into the snow, landing on his back, hammering the wind out of him.

Darkness and raw pain from his face rushed over him, and for a moment all he could do was lie there, cawing for breath, slowly dragging the cold air into his lungs.

"Damn," he moaned and, trembling, he pushed up on his shoulder and touched his face gently. It was wet with blood.

"Not bad," he told himself. "Not bad."

Rolling over onto his stomach, he looked down at the ground. He had to get the rifle and— Blinking, he looked at the ground again. He could barely make anything out.

Everything was white, gray, and black, but there was no form to it.

"Oh, my—" he murmured and the realization jerked through him like he'd been kicked.

He was blind.

CHAPTER 14

Rufe and Maggie plunged down and around the shelf to cover. Bringing the horses around, Rufe shoved the reins into the woman's hands then knelt down and reloaded his Hawken.

Finishing, he reeled, running back along the shelf, crouching as the line of rock blended into the slope, then lay down as he reached the end of it, turning his rifle toward the Indians. He fired quickly, reloaded and fired again.

Pouring powder and shot in the Hawken, he kept his

eyes upslope, waiting for Mattick to move before he fired again.

He rammed the load home and replaced the rod, still waiting. There was no sign of Mattick.

The old man's eyes narrowed questioningly, then he frowned. "Damn . . ." he sighed. He had no choice. "Mattick—" he shouted, his voice echoing. "Mattick, call out—"

In the rocks, Lake's head jerked up at the sound of Rufe's voice. Fighting the panic thickening in his throat, he forced himself to answer.

"Rufe," he yelled. "I'm blinded. Keep firing."

"Mattick—"

"Goddammit, Rufe," he raged. "Shut up and keep firing." Silence. Then a gunshot. From Rufe.

Pushing up on his knees, Lake shoved his hands out and around him, searching for the Henry. He didn't have much time. The shouting had given away his position. If he was going to get out of there, it was going to have to be quick. His hands scraped over the rocks and through the snow, but he couldn't feel a damn thing. His hands were cold anyway, and the buckskin gloves made everything feel the same.

Tearing the gloves off, he tried again. An arrow ripped through the rocks. Then a flurry of them.

"Bastards. . . ." he growled, his hands still moving. He almost wished for gunfire. At least that way he knew what was coming.

His hands began to rise. He was on the downside of the sink. Turning, he crawled back to the opposite side, his hands raking the ground, beginning to numb from the cold. And he touched something metal.

His fingers closed around it, and he almost laughed. It was the Henry.

Kneeling down, Lake pulled the Henry to him, until the barrel touched his knees, then he reached under his coat, and tugged his shirttail out. Gripping it, he wrenched a tear in it, then pulled it on around until he had taken a strip off the bottom.

Picking up the rifle, he knotted one end of the cloth around the barrel, and secured the other end through the lever ring and around the grip.

After testing the makeshift sling, he shoved his arm through, then looped it around his head and let it hang on his back.

Nodding, he cupped his hands in front of his mouth and blew into them. His gloves, he remembered, and another wash of arrows ripped the air above him.

The hell with the gloves, he thought, and started crawling. Pushing down into a crouching position, he fumbled, crawl-walking his way across the sink, cracking his shin on a rock.

"Damn," he growled, and scrambled up the sheet of sandstone, down the other side into the twisting of rock. Having moved, he felt safer and he hesitated, waiting for Rufe's next shot trying to set a picture in his mind of the escarpment below him. The sandstone outcropping, the boulder, the passage between them. Below the boulder it was clear to the piñons. Then clear again to the shelf.

Rufe's shot would be his only bearing. He had to place everything else according to it. Leaning forward on his toes, he primed himself to run.

The Hawken crashed. Lake fixed on the shot, then it began to echo away. Disappearing in the crystal air. Down. To his far right. He nodded. He was headed in the right direction.

Vaulting up, he wound through the sandstone, feeling his way with his hands, picking up speed as he moved. He was headed down. Angling.

Slamming into a waist-high rock, he scraped his knees and right arm, but kept moving. Sliding along it. Dropping into an open space, across it into another slab of sandstone.

His fingers were raw and numb from the snow and stone. But he kept them against the rocks. Pushing himself. Nearly running.

The ground dipped under him and staggering forward, his foot slipped in the snow, throwing him headfirst into the ground. Tumbling. Ramming to a halt as his hip caught a rock. Pulling himself up on his elbows, he shook his head.

"Gettin' a little tired of this—" he sighed under his breath, then checking to see if he still had the Henry, he shoved himself to his feet and started through the rocks.

Rufe put another ball up the slope. Lake's head came up and a tremor of relief brushed his lips. He was headed right.

Then scraping through a narrow passage he was suddenly in the open. His hands groped for another rock, but there were none. He inched his foot forward and the ground dropped abruptly under him.

Getting down on his hands and knees, he crawled across the drop, and raised his eyes straining to see. In front and above him was a huge blur. For a moment, he thought he'd gotten worse, then looking down, the blur gave way to silver darkness.

His eyes jerked up, and he made his way across the open space and reaching out, touched the blur in front of him. It was the boulder. He was in the draw between it and the sandstone outcropping.

Staying low, nearly lying down on his side, he slipped down the gravel and snow, his eyes staying on the blur next to him. It eased away from him slowly, then was gone.

He was completely in the open now. Flattening himself against the ground, he lay as still as he could, and swept his eyes over the slope below him.

It was nothing but a void. Trembling, he pressed himself into the snow and gravel.

He wished like hell he could relieve his kidneys. The tension from them ached through his body, and his hands were brittle with cold. Pulling his hands up, he cupped them to his mouth, breathing on them, and tried to get the pain in his kidneys out of his mind. The more he thought about it, the worse it got.

"Thinking again." He frowned.

Flexing his fingers, he touched the butt of the Henry, then lifted himself away from the ground and began sliding down the slope. Pushing himself with his hands, he raked through the snow, catching himself with his feet, then used his hands again. Sliding into the darkness.

The Hawken crashed, the report rolling up the slope. Lake jerked to a halt. The shot was off to the right. He was moving away from Rufe.

Frustration and anger surged through him, and gathering his hands into fists, he forced himself to calm down. He had to move, not think. Thinking would kill him. Swallowing cold air, he turned, crawling horizontally across the incline.

Another shot cracked the black air, and above him, Lake heard a scream, then the slice of arrows latticing the darkness, whorling around him.

He rammed down into the snow. The rake of arrows ebbed away as quickly as they had come, and lifting himself on his hands, he scrambled across the dark face. Rufe fired again. Almost directly below him.

Shoving down into a half-standing position, Lake pushed out and away from the slope, dropping down and catching himself with his feet. He was moving quickly now, scraping across sandstone and through the snow.

"This way," Rufe shouted, and Lake angled toward the voice, plummeting into darkness, slamming his knees and hands on rocks, his fingers clawing the snow, trying to keep him from dropping too fast. His boot skimmed over rock and sank into snow. Then nothing.

His foot plunged through the snow, and for a split second, he was suspended in mid-air. Tipping backward. Reeling, he tried to get his hands around to break his fall, but he slammed into his side and he could hear the sound of something crushing beneath him. Tumbling, something rattled around him. His hands pounded into the snow, trying to catch himself, but he was still hopelessly falling. Careening down the slope like a child on a sled.

Flailing, he rammed his fingers into the ground, tearing them over the sandstone and gravel, finally driving them into the snow and dirt, slowly dragging himself to a halt.

Exhausted, his breath rasped through him, raw and cold, and he lay still for a minute, trying to get up enough strength to move again.

"Mattick," Rufe called. "Keep comin'. You're past the trees. Maybe sixty more feet."

And Maggie's voice. "Mr. Mattick—please—"

Their voices tugged his head up, and he tried to move, but he felt as if he was stitched together with water and sleep.

He slumped back to the ground breathing snow and darkness. Deep in him something rustled, but he felt as if motion was a dream lost, slipping away from him. He had to get up. He had to—

Then suddenly there were hands on him, and the smell of tobacco, and horse and leather. The hands pulled him up and he tried to hit whoever it was.

"Goddammit, Mattick," the old man growled, "let's get goin'."

Sitting up, Lake's hand brushed against something ragged on his side. Pieces of—

"Jesus—" he whispered, groping.

It was his cartridge box. That's what he'd heard break when he fell. And the pieces of metal had been his shells. Frantically, he turned to the ground, his hands combing the snow.

"Mattick," the old man growled, "what the hell—?"

"My ammunition—all of it gone—"

The hands jerked him around again. "We ain't got the time," he said.

And Lake was up. Walking. Leaning into the old man. Then running. Crashing down the slope. The old man guiding him. Moving together. Arrows cut the air around them, but he and Rufe kept going. Down and around a rock.

"The shelf is just a couple more—" the old man said, then his wind barked out of him, and he slammed into Lake.

"Rufe," he cried, and both of them went down, plowing into the snow.

Lake reached around, feeling the old man. "Rufe—"

"All . . . right . . ." the old man answered thickly. "Let's go—"

Standing, Lake helped Rufe up.

"Straight down, not far now," the old man said. "Come on, dammit," he growled. They pushed out, and the old man felt heavy against him, and slow.

"Rufe—"

"Dammit," he snapped. "Will you shut up and move—?"

———◆———

Maggie had seen them go down, but it wasn't until they came around the shelf that she saw the arrow through the old man's shoulder.

"Rufe," she whispered, rushing to him.

The old man slumped down, and Mattick sank to his knees beside him.

"What is it?" he asked Maggie.

"I'm hit," Rufe answered. "Through the muscle on the collarbone. Now help me up and let's get out of here."

"But the arrow—" Maggie began.

"Not now," the old man said, reaching out to her. "Let's get out of here." Maggie stared at him.

"Mrs. Calder, goddammit, move your butt."

Blinking, she reached down and pulled him up. Then Lake. Stumbling, she helped them to the horses and got them mounted, then pulled herself into the saddle behind Lake.

Leaning in the saddle, the old man turned his horse out, and looked back up the ridge.

"The Indians—?" Lake asked.

"Comin'"—the old man frowned—"and comin' hard." He looked to Maggie. "It's yours again, ma'am," he swallowed.

Nodding, she wheeled her horse out, leading them to the bottom of the slope, then out into the flat.

CHAPTER 15

It seemed to Lake that they had been riding a long time when the sun finally came. A brittle shard of nameless color dividing black and white. Chanting form and time. Webbing like a memory, then exploding brightness through fragment mirrors of snow engulfing the riders in a wash of light.

On the running horse, Lake pulled his head down, hiding it in his collar. The light blinded him worse than the darkness. It was as if he was floating in a freezing sun.

"Slow 'em," he heard Rufe say, and he felt his horse

shorten his step, the animal's weariness cawing through his breathing.

Behind Lake, Rufe eased his blue in, the pain from the arrow still throbbing through his left shoulder, down his arm, and in his trunk. Glancing up at it, the old man realized he'd almost gotten used to the head jiggling beside his face. Now though looking at it, he could see the blood on it, and that bothered him. Bringing his eyes forward, he saw Maggie looking at him.

"Not now," he said, answering the question in her eyes. He nodded at Lake.

"How you doin', Lieutenant?"

"Can't make out a damn thing."

"Sun?"

Mattick nodded. A slight smile touched Rufe's lips. "If the sun's botherin' you, you ain't blind."

"There's always a silver lining," Lake commented sourly.

Rufe's grin widened. "Ain't there though." The grin sighed into laughter. "Damned if we ain't in fine shape. Me with a shaft of wood stuck in me. The soldier half blind. The horses about to drop, and no more shells for that fancy brass rifle. You got any cartridges left at all?"

Lake shook his head. "Just what's in the rifle. Four, maybe."

The old man unstrung the canteen from his saddle horn and uncorked it.

"Hold out your hand," he told Mattick.

The ex-soldier stretched out his hand and Rufe poured a few drops of water into his palm, and Lake splashed it in his eyes and blinked.

"Help any?" Rufe asked.

"Some." Lake nodded. "Stings like hell."

"Yeah." Rufe frowned. "Damn canteen water always has a funny taste to it." He corked the canteen and hung it back on the horn. "Likely irritatin' those eyes. Probably best to let time and your own eye water work on'em. Flush'em with fresh when we get to New Eden."

Lake nodded his agreement and Rufe turned, looking back. The sun on the snow was a holocaust of light. He couldn't see a damn thing either.

"Hell," he sighed, and shaking his head, he sat around front and they rounded a small knoll, then started up a hogback.

The sun eased farther into the sky, drawing the sharp brightness from the snow as it climbed, giving form back to the land.

Under him, Rufe's horse struggled up the slope, and the mountain man found himself having to hold onto the saddle horn to keep his balance, and he felt every lurch of the blue in his shoulder.

Stiffly, he turned, looking back again. He was better able to make out the flats they were leaving now. There was no sign of the Absorakas.

Lifting his eyes, he tried to see the escarpment, but it was hidden by the roll of the horizon.

He frowned. "Damn prairie."

Maggie's eyes came around. "What?"

"Nothin'," the old man growled. "Just what looks flat out here ain't really flat." He turned in the saddle with difficulty, and flinched with pain.

"Mr. Kitrel?" Maggie asked. "Can we do something about that shoulder now?"

The old man nodded. "Guess we better." He swallowed

and spurred the blue out, topping the hogback. They angled along the crest to a spine of low rocks pushing out of the snow, and Rufe eased down the opposite slope, then pulled in beneath the rocks.

Dismounting awkwardly, he sat down on a rock while Maggie stood down, and helped Lake to the ground. Then she turned to Rufe. The arrow had penetrated clear through the old man's shoulder.

"Take the shaft in both hands," he instructed her. "On the feather side. Break it as close to the shoulder as you can without puttin' too much pressure on me."

Maggie did as she was told. Grasping the wood with both hands. And hesitated.

Rufe looked at her. "Well—"

"Just—" She shook her head. "Nothing."

Rufe could feel her hands tighten on the shaft, holding it, and the pressure bending down on it. A shock of pain jerked through him, and it seemed like she was taking a long time.

"Mrs. . . . Calder . . ." he growled, and the shaft snapped, cracking like a distant shot.

The pain fluttered in him, thick and hot in his throat, and he nodded.

"Now . . . take . . . the other piece and pull . . . it out," he whispered tightly. "Do it quick."

He was turning his head away, when he felt her hand close on the shaft again. Then jerked. For a second it was like somebody had torn the muscle out of his shoulder.

Resting back, he let his breath ease through him for a moment, and Maggie tore a length of cloth from her blouse sleeve and slipped it inside his shirt and coat until it was covering both openings.

"I'm obliged," he said shakily, and sat forward, then stood up.

"Mr. Kitrel," Maggie protested. "You can't ride now—"

"Not goin' to," the old man said. "Goin' back up there—" He pointed to the top of the hogback.

"Why—?"

"To have a look-see. Now help me up there. I'm a tad wobbley legged." Maggie frowned, then helped him the few feet up the incline. He nodded his appreciation.

"I can get it now. Go on back down with the lieutenant."

As she edged back down the incline, Rufe turned through the rocks. His shoulder was heavy and stiff, but better.

Coming through the rocks to the open slope, he sank to his knees, and using his good arm, he stretched out, lying flat on his belly. There was still nothing out there.

He frowned, an uneasiness razoring his stomach. He could see back maybe fifteen miles. They shouldn't be that far back.

A rueful smile touched his lips. If he had fifteen miles on them, he shouldn't be complaining.

"Must be gettin' contrary—" he sighed and pushed himself up, using his good arm. Hesitating, he cast a last look at the flats.

"Sure like to know where you boys are." He frowned, the uneasiness spreading. Turning, he walked back through the rocks and down the slope to Maggie and Lake.

"See 'em?" Lake asked.

"'Fraid not," Rufe answered, and helped Lake up, then let Maggie guide him to his horse.

When they were mounted, Lake's head came around. "Nothin'?" he asked.

Rufe shook his head. "Not a sign."

The ex-soldier shook his head. "That don't make sense. Maybe the escarpment did stop'em."

"I don't think so," Rufe said, then shook his head. "Hell, I don't know. That's the whole goddamn trouble." He frowned and nudged the blue. "I just don't know."

CHAPTER 16

They bottomed the ridge and moved out across the flats.

Rufe felt as if he'd been riding for a hundred years. How many days we been at this, he wondered, then smiled weakly, realizing it had only been about twenty-four hours since they had ridden down into that canyon.

Funny, he mused, how even time got twisted on this damn prairie. Twenty-four hours. A lifetime in the smile of a woman or the glint of sunlight on a knife edge. Maybe this was the way you lived forever. . . .

He rubbed his face. Gettin' tired, he thought. Addled.

Weariness bled through him like a whisper. Numbing him. Pressing the weight of sleep into his eyelids.

Only the motion of the horse beneath him, fingering the pain in his shoulder, kept him awake. That and wondering where the Absorakas were.

Glancing back, he frowned. Something was out of whack, he knew that. Like seeing a face you knew, but the name wouldn't come.

Blinking, he shook his head trying to push away the uneasy feeling and the sleepiness. Tired, he thought again. Maybe that was it. He nodded. Maybe he was just tired.

He looked at Lake. He was slumped forward in the saddle, his head nodding. Rufe smiled. Damned if the lieutenant wasn't asleep.

"Wish I could do that," Maggie said. "I keep losing my balance."

"One of the benefits of war, I reckon. You learn to sleep when you can. And how to keep your balance doin' it. Course it only comes in handy at times like this."

Maggie's eyes went forward. "How much farther do you think?"

Rufe looked to the peaks. "Till a little before noon, likely. Not sure. I only been there the one time."

"What religion are they—the people at New Eden?"

Rufe thought for a moment, then shook his head. "Told me, but I disremember. One of them groups that keep to themselves. Didn't like likker or dancin'."

"I guess that's why they never came to the Post."

Rufe nodded. "Wanted to do it all themselves. Each to his own, I reckon."

"Yes," she agreed, and stretched. "Right now I'd give a hundred dollars for a bed."

"I'll take your rein and you wrap the lieutenant's around your horn there. Now set your feet in the stirrups and your hand on the horn. Close your eyes, and your hand touchin' the horn. Now if you go to one side or the other, your hand ought to talk to your brain. Never take the place of a bed, but you'll doze a little."

———————————◆————————————

The morning slipped slowly away. The three riders drifted between the low hills like errant pieces of color, leaving scrawls in the white.

Lake and Maggie dozed intermittently, and Rufe took the lead. The pain throbbed in his shoulder, and reaching inside his coat and shirt he touched the compress Maggie had put on the wound. It was wet.

Frowning, he nodded. He was still bleeding. Not much, but he was bleeding. New Eden couldn't be far now, he thought. They would take care of it there.

Beneath him, the blue moved steadily; wearily and awake, Rufe dreamed of sleep. And food. Elk steak and buffalo liver. Great roasts dripping hot fat.

"Damn," he grumbled and reaching in his pocket, he withdrew a pemmican cake. Biting in, he frowned. It was dry and chewy. He still thought of buffalo roasts.

Remembering. The good days before the fur trade had died out. Days of the boys. The companyeros. Lads bringing in their furs to the companies. Then the rendezvous. An excuse to get drunk for five or six days.

He smiled. All those fine boys. Gone now, most of them. The smile faded, and he touched his shoulder again.

Good thing that settlement was coming up or he'd be joining them.

He frowned. Maybe they were the smart ones. Like Dick. At least he'd got to pick his spot.

And there was something to be said for that.

CHAPTER 17

The sun pulled higher in the sky. Lake dozed, then awoke and dozed again, never sleeping for more than a few minutes at a time. Finally he gave it up, and bringing his eyes up, he realized he could make out shapes now. Maggie, the light in her hair, and Rufe looking at him.

"Better?" the old man asked.

Lake nodded. "Yeah."

Rufe smiled. "That natural eye water's cleanin' 'em," he said. "Get some fresh water at that settlement and they'll be good as new."

Next to Lake, Maggie stirred in the saddle and looked at the two men sleepily.

"How'd you do?" Lake asked.

"Mr. Kitrel was right. It'll never take the place of a bed," Maggie said, holding back a yawn.

"No," Lake agreed. "Guess it won't."

"I don't understand." She shook her head. "How do you do it?"

"Practice."

Maggie looked at him, nearly staring. "You must have been very good at it," she said.

"Sleeping?"

"No, being a soldier."

He nodded. "I was. You either become very good at it or you get killed."

"Were you a career officer?"

"No," he replied and smiled.

"What is it?" she asked.

"Just . . . strange, that anyone would think I was career Army."

"Why? You seem very much like a soldier," Maggie said.

Lake's eyes came around, and he was silent for a moment. "Do I?" he asked, a hint of amazement in his voice, then he nodded. "Yes, I guess I would. Odd . . ."

"Why?"

Lake's eyes came back to her, and he shrugged. "I don't know. How people become the opposite of what they start out to be. Mirror images. I was reading to be a teacher before the war."

Rufe's head came up at that. "A teacher?"

Lake nodded.

"You mean a schoolmaster?"

Lake nodded again. Rufe shook his head disbelievingly.

"You just don't seem like no schoolteacher. How come you to take it up? You fond of the little ones?"

"No," Lake answered. "Books."

"How the hell—Scuse me, ma'am—did you end up in that war?"

Lake smiled suddenly. "By trying to steal a watermelon."

Rufe grinned and so did Maggie.

"By what?" Maggie asked.

Lake nodded. "I was fourteen years old and on my own." The smile faded. "Folks died when I was ten. My father hauling freight in Virginia, by a highwayman, and my mother a few months later of nothing but too much work and too little food. Relatives came and took my brother and sister. Uncle tried to take me too, but I ran off. Got along by stealing mostly. Worked some, when I could, but I always got by. One way or another I got by, and in a lot of ways it wasn't a bad life."

"I'd think it would be terrible. Being so alone," Maggie said.

Lake shook his head. "No," he said. "I liked it."

"Don't you ever need other people?"

Lake looked at her. "Gallagher asked me that same question. More than once."

"Who?" Maggie asked.

"Michael Patrick Gallagher," Lake answered. "The man that caught me stealing the watermelon. He was a big man—a blacksmith—and he turned me everyway but loose. Then he took me back to the rooms he had in the barn at the edge of a little town called Two Springs, on the eastern border of Illinois. Fed me and put me to bed. I tried running away the next day, but he caught me and said he'd throw me in jail if I tried it again. I lived with him there for three years. Worked my tail off and taught me to read and write. I guess that's why I stayed."

"A blacksmith?" Maggie asked.

"Yeah." Lake nodded. "A blacksmith. Self-educated. Think he was always a little surprised how I took to it."

"Is he the one that persuaded you to be a teacher?" Maggie asked.

Lake looked at her, his eyes darkening slightly, and he shook his head. "No. It was my idea. When I told him, he said I shouldn't do it."

Maggie frowned. "Why?"

"Said I didn't care enough about people. And I'd missed the most important thing in the books. That somebody out there felt the way I did." Lake smiled tightly. "'Lame-brain,' he used to call me, when he was frustrated with me, which was most of the time. 'That's the whole point.' Always shaking his head, telling me to loosen up. Quit being so damn logical, and try laughing at myself ever' once in a while."

"Not bad advice," Rufe put in, then smiled. "Remember back at the rendezvous sometimes, the boys'd laugh more at the bad times than anything else. Likely all that kept us goin'."

"Still"—Lake shrugged—"logic and planning are the only way you get anywhere."

Rufe smiled. "Depends on where you're tryin' to go."

"Where is Gallagher now?" Maggie asked.

Lake's eyes jerked to hers, staring for a moment, then he looked away. "Dead," he answered. "One of the fifty-seven killed in Tennessee."

The horses moved under them carrying them along a low line of hills. Lake rode in silence, but he could feel Maggie's eyes on him.

"What happened?" she finally asked.

"Why?" he snapped.

She blinked at his sudden anger. "What—"

"Why do you want to know?"

Maggie thought for a moment, her eyes softening. "I'm not sure," she answered. "I just want to understand."

"Understand what?"

"You."

He blinked. "Why?" he asked, not trying to hide the surprise in his voice.

She smiled. "That's the part I'm not sure of," she said and shrugged. "Actually, it's probably a little selfish. Maybe a lot. Back there, after the river, you talked about control. I guess that's what I'd like to understand. That, and you and Mr. Kitrel are the only two men that have listened to me like I had something to say." The smile brushed her lips again. "You're both still prejudiced, but you listen."

Rufe looked at Lake. "Did she just badmouth us?"

"In a round-about way," Lake grinned, then looked at her for a moment, his gaze gentling until the smile was gone, and he nodded.

"Quincy was the mayor of the town," he said. "When the war broke out, he formed a company along with the other small towns around there. First time I really re-member him, he was standing up there on the courthouse steps, drunk, hoisting glasses with those that joined. It was going to be over in ninety days, he said."

Lake frowned. "It wasn't. Far from it. He came back six months later. Where they were paying men before, they were conscripting them now. Went through town gather-ing up all the young men that hadn't joined. I was one of them. Gallagher tried to join, but he was too old. Too old for them. But I was sworn in and marched off."

"Why not just take out some dark night?" Rufe put in.

"I thought about it," Lake nodded. "Except that they shot deserters on the spot. That or the Rebs got hold of you and threw you in a camp or put you in one of their own companies with a gun to your head. No, I was better off where I was."

"Did your friends feel the same?" Maggie asked. "Maybe all of you—"

"I didn't have any friends," Lake cut in. "In order to survive, that was the first rule. You didn't get close to anybody. I had learned that before I met Gallagher, and I learned it again after our first battle. Friends, the enemy— they were all the same. In order to survive, you cut your-self away from everything and become the best at what you're doing. Being a soldier, learning to kill, was a skill like any other. I guess that's why Quincy made me an officer. Because I followed orders and because I had some education. It was almost a joke. I had become exactly the opposite of what I had started out to be.

"I might just have made it too"—Lake swallowed—"if it hadn't been for Gallagher. It seemed like the war went on forever, and as it did, the replacements got older and older. Finally one of them was Gallagher. Joined us in Tennessee. Came walking up to me one day with that saber in his hand." Lake touched the weapon beneath his leg. "Said it was a genuine Chicopee, and it had cost him seven dollars and fifty cents and I was damn well going to take it. Then he got that big stupid grin on his face. 'When all else fails'—he winked—'charge!'"

Lake trembled slightly, his hands tightening on the reins. "Damn fool had joined," he said. "And a month later he was dead."

"How?" Maggie asked.

Lake frowned. "Quincy had heard there were a few Rebs holding out in a valley near the Mississippi, and he decided he was going to clean them out. He wanted more glory I guess. Maybe a promotion. The war was nearly over, and whatever he was going to do, he had to do it fast.

"The other officers and I tried to talk him out of it, but he was drunk as usual and wouldn't listen."

Lake's jaw tightened. "It was stupid. The whole damn thing. He sent my platoon and another straight into the valley. There was no cover, and the Rebs had the high ground. But he sent us in anyway, knowing it was wrong. All of us knew. . . ." He swallowed, trembling. "The Rebs got fifty-seven of us. Gallagher was one of them.

"I was one of the lucky ones. Took a ball in the leg. I was discharged from the hospital the week the war ended. Quincy had been discharged instead of court-martialed and word was he'd headed west.

"I drew my back pay, and came after him. He wasn't

hard to follow. I checked into the freight, stagecoach, and wagon-train headquarters in St. Louis and found he'd come up the Missouri, then out here. A week ago I heard a freight driver at Shell Landing talking about a drunken ex-cavalry officer at Cunningham's, waiting for the snow to melt in the mountains so he could cross to California."

A silence eased through the ex-soldier and his hands trembled. "That's why I have to get there. And get there quick. I have to be there before the party he's traveling with starts across the mountains. If he makes it to California, I might never find him."

The horses pushed down and across a dry wash, and Lake shook his head. "Funny . . ." he sighed.

"What, Mr. Mattick?"

"I haven't talked that much since I used to argue with Gallagher," he said, then was quiet again.

———◆———

They rode down a long roll of hills and as the sun was nearing noon they rounded a small knoll and Rufe pulled his horse in.

"Be damned," the old man whispered.

"What is it?"

"The settlement," Maggie answered. "New Eden."

Lake strained to see, but could only make out a dark scrawl in the white.

"Ha—" The old man laughed and slapped Lake on the shoulder. "Like to run these animals in, damned if I wouldn't, but I reckon we better walk 'em. How 'bout that, ma'am?"

Maggie nodded. "Yes"—she swallowed—"how 'bout that?"

They nudged their horses out, trotting into the open, across the open ground.

Squinting, Lake began to make out lines, then the walls of the stockade, and the gate. Next to him, the old man began to rein in his horse slightly.

"Funny—" he said. His voice quiet. Taut.

The edge in Rufe's voice tugged Lake's head around. "What—?"

"The gate," Rufe said. "It's open. Has been the whole way in." He looked at Mattick. "That Henry might do me a little more good than you right now," he said.

Lake nodded and unstrung it from his back and handed it to Rufe. Taking it, the old man slipped his Hawken into its boot, then lifted the Henry.

"Take it easy," the old man said and moved out.

They crossed the ground to the gate slowly. Reaching out, Rufe pulled it the rest of the way open, and all three stood staring inside.

"My God," Maggie finally whispered. "There's no one here."

CHAPTER 18

Rufe led them inside the deserted settlement and they dismounted. Maggie stepped down and helped Lake to the ground.

"I'm all right," he nodded and blinked, trying to clear his eyes. He could make out small low buildings. An ice house. Root cellar against the far wall. Corrals next to that. All empty.

"Where the hell is everybody?" he finally asked.

"Gone," Rufe answered simply.

Maggie shook her head. "But where—?"

"I don't know," the old man frowned. "Happens like this sometimes. There just ain't no answers. Used to be the boys would just get together for a rendezvous and somebody just wouldn't show up. Like Buford Tull. Went out one winter and never come back. Never found no traces of him. He was just gone. Like these folks."

"But there must have been over a hundred people here. You just can't lose a hundred people."

"Sure you can," the old man nodded. "You two rest a minute," he said. "Think there's a stream down behind those houses. Get some water for the lieutenant's eyes."

As the old man walked out across the settlement, Maggie led the horses and pointed Lake to the porch of one of the houses. Sitting down, they looked around the compound.

"What do we do now?" Maggie asked.

"Head for Cunningham's," Lake said immediately. "Only place to go now."

"Yes"—Maggie nodded—"I suppose it is."

Across the compound, Rufe came around a house and walked back toward them. Coming by the horses, he took his canteen from his saddle.

"This'll have to do," he said, sitting down beside Lake.

"What about the stream?" Lake asked.

"Hold out your hands," Rufe said. "It's gone too," he answered pouring the water. "Dried up. There's another one, but it's five or six miles on south."

Lake washed his eyes, wincing slightly. "Damn," he whispered.

"Sting?" Rufe asked.

"A little," Lake nodded and dried his face with his sleeve.

"That's probably why they left," he said. "The stream drying up."

"Maybe," Rufe nodded. "That's as good an answer as any if you need one. You want more?"

Lake shook his head, and the old man corked the canteen and, laying it down, he brought the Henry up.

"Reckon we better see how many chances we got," he said.

Jacking the lever, a shell jumped from the chamber. Rufe repeated the action until the Henry was empty.

"Three," Lake counted.

The old man nodded, and uncapping the loading barrel, he began sliding the shells back in. When he was finished, he pushed to his feet and walked into the open.

Standing alone, he lifted his eyes to the mountains. Clouds rushed over the peaks, and a wind rustled the snow. The old man looked at them for a long time, then lowered his gaze to his left arm. Fresh blood was darkening his sleeve.

"Old Dick," he whispered and nodded as he turned back to Maggie and Lake. "Let's move," he said and walked to the horses.

Mounting up, they rode back across the yard and out the gate, and Rufe turned his blue toward the mountains.

Behind him, Lake pulled in his horse and looked toward the plains.

"Where you going?" he asked Rufe.

The old man reined in and looked at Lake. "Up there," Rufe gestured toward the mountains.

"Cunningham's is the other way," Lake said.

Rufe nodded. "I know. We're goin' through the mountains."

"Why? The quickest way is—"

"The quickest ain't necessarily the best. You'll get to Cunningham's," the old man said. "It'll take a little more time, but you'll get there."

"I can't afford the time," Lake snapped. "Quincy could be gone even now. I've got to—"

"Bullshit," Rufe barked. "The time to have done somethin' was back there in Tennessee. If'n you'd done what you knew was right, and not followed Quincy's order, your friend might still be alive. Killing Quincy ain't gonna change that."

Lake quieted, staring at the old man. "Rufe—"

"Quincy was wrong, but so were you. You been wrong all the way down the line," the old man said and raised the Henry. "Now we're goin' up, and I ain't gonna talk about it no more. Move," he ordered the ex-soldier.

Lake stared at the old man a moment longer, then wordlessly, he spurred his horse out and took the lead.

CHAPTER 19

It took them an hour to cross the flats and start up the foothills. Lake was still in the lead. Then Maggie. Rufe brought up the rear.

Looking down at his arm again, the old man shook his head. The blood had soaked through his coat at the shoulder and upper sleeve.

It wasn't bad. But steady. It would be worse tomorrow. And the next day. And the one after that.

Easing around, he looked back. There was no sign of

the Absorakas. Frowning, he shook his head. Where the hell are they? he wondered. They—

Beneath him, the blue swung his head up suddenly sniffing the wind. Ahead of him, Maggie's horse turned out and Maggie had to jerk him back around. Lake's Morgan nickered softly.

"What's wrong with them?" Maggie asked.

"Whoa." Rufe tightened the rein on his animal and nudged him on. "Been a while since they had water," he said, "and they can smell that other stream. Only water around here. Least the only this side of that bluff we come down."

"Should we—?"

"Just keep movin'," Rufe said.

———◆———

They pushed on through the steepening foothills and started up the first slope of the mountains. It was a long, gradual rise, a lower peak rising out of the hills, lifting to the range building above them.

A little over halfway up the slope, Rufe eased around and looked back the way they'd come, his eyes following the scatterings of their tracks.

Below them, the wind rustled a mist from the snow, blending the hills and the prairie, making them seem like mist too. Like a place a half a world away. Someplace he might have imagined as a boy. And he was a stranger there. They all were.

His hand tightened on the saddle horn and he frowned. At least it wouldn't be down on that damn prairie; he nodded and turned front in the saddle.

They skirted around the side of the peak and pulled over a low ridge, then dropped down into a narrow sloping valley.

They angled down it, cutting across an open area toward a stand of pine and spruce that spread as it went down the valley and covered several small hills at the lower end of the hollow.

Pushing into the timber, they started up another ridge, and Rufe looked back again. This ridge was a little higher than the first. Through the trees, he could make out the lay of the valley and the opposite ridge clearly.

Turning, he looked to the top of the ridge. About fifty yards from the crest to the timber, he gauged. He nodded. It was a good place. At least it would do.

The horses pulled to the top of the rise, angling into a stand of broken rocks, and Rufe felt a weight growing in his chest like thickening lead.

It was time. Clearing his throat, he called to Lake.

"Haul it in," he said in a gravelly voice.

The young man swung his shoulders around. "Why?"

Rufe's lips tightened. "Just pull'em in," he ordered the other man softly and drew the blue up.

Wheeling, Lake and Maggie rode back to him. Rufe's good hand closed around the saddle horn and, gripping it tightly, he slipped his leg over the saddle and lowered himself to the ground slowly, then sat down in an outcropping of close clustered rocks.

Lake and Maggie dismounted next to him, and Rufe raised his eyes. A near angry frown was pulling Lake's mouth.

"What the hell you doin'," he snapped. "We've got to keep movin'—"

The old man shook his head. "You've got to keep movin'," he corrected Lake. "I'm stayin' here."

Lake's eyes narrowed, the anger softening on his mouth.

"What—?"

"I didn't stutter, boy."

"You can't—" Maggie shook her head. "We—"

"Ma'am," Rufe cut her off, "this wound is bleedin' on me. I'll slow you. I'm already doin' it. I'm not goin' to make it anyway."

"Mr. Kitrel—"

"Dammit, Mrs. Calder," he sighed. "We've run out of options." Reaching out, Rufe touched her hand. "Ma'am, I'd rather have it this way. Least it's my spot and my terms. Not like a bled-out buck's that's run out all his fight. This way I'll give the Absoraka what for."

Lake knelt down and nodded. "That's why you brought us up here. So you could hold them a little while and give us more time."

"You're catchin' on." Rufe winked.

"The settlement would have been a better place. You might even have—"

"I didn't like it down there." Rufe frowned. "Not on that damn prairie." He pointed south across the slope. "You head that way," he said. "You'll hit that other stream I was tellin' you about. Follow it down, back out on the prairie, it'll lead you right to Cunningham's. You ought to make it. You'll have an extra horse."

Lake nodded. "Rufe, what you said back down there, I've been thinking—"

The old man held up the Henry. "Mind gettin' me my piece?"

Lake shook his head. "The Henry would be better."

"Rather have my own," the old man said.

Nodding and taking the rifle, Lake walked to the blue, slipped the Hawken from its boot, and returned to the old man.

"I'm obliged." Rufe nodded, taking the rifle, then looked at the ex-soldier. "You know, me and old Dick used to talk about headin' back into the Leyenda when we got the money. Just wanted you to know, even if you are kinda crossways about some things, I'd've liked to had you along."

Lake looked down at the old man, staring, silent for a moment. Then nodding, he turned and took Maggie's arm.

"Mr. Mattick," she protested, "we—"

"Like he said. We've run out of options."

They mounted and Lake took the blue's reins, then turned the Morgan down the slope, angling toward the trees at the bottom of the valley. Maggie hesitated, looking back at Rufe.

"Good-by, Mrs. Calder," the old man said.

Her eyes stayed on him a moment longer, then she shook her head helplessly. "I don't . . . like this. . . ." The tears were in her throat now.

The old man smiled. "I don't either."

Her lips trembled, smiling slightly, the tears wet on her cheeks. "Damn," she shouted, strapping her horse out, following Lake.

Rufe watched them until they sank into the trees and were gone. He stared after them a long time, the gnaw of loneliness and fear stretching through him. For a moment, he nearly called out to them. But he didn't. He couldn't do that. . . . Trembling, he pulled his eyes around, looking downslope. His hand tightened on the old Hawken.

"If you ain't whipped the devil by now, Dick, hold on. I'm gonna come give you a little help."

CHAPTER 20

Coming around a small knoll, Lake heard the water, then saw it. He and Maggie crossed a sandbar, and Lake pulled the Morgan in at the edge of the water. The horses dipped their heads to drink.

"Getting down?" Lake asked.

Maggie shook her head. Her thoughts were still with Rufe.

Nodding, Lake handed her the reins to the Morgan and the blue. "Want to wash my eyes again," he said and dismounted. Kneeling beside the stream, he lay the Henry down, then scooped water up in his face, flushing his eyes gently.

"How are they?" Maggie asked.

"Doin' better," he said and was dipping his hands into the water again, when he heard something. His head came up.

The sound rasped again. Faint, but there. Something scraping rock. Downstream. Just beyond a hill that made a bend in the creek. Lake's eyes came up and around to Maggie. She was already dismounting.

Picking up the Henry, he turned to her, pushing her down gently, then looked back to the bend. Something clattered on the rocks, splashing water. Lake waited. The sound came again.

He looked at Maggie. "Sounds like just one," he whispered. Maggie nodded.

Lake thought for a moment, then handed Maggie the Henry. "Stay here," he said and tugged his knife from the sheath on his belt.

Maggie's eyes widened slightly when she realized he was leaving her. "I—"

"Got no choice." Lake frowned and bringing his knife up he pushed out, stepping quietly. Slowly. Leaving the woman behind.

Watching him, Maggie knew that in a moment she would be alone. Her hand tightened on the brass of the Henry and she felt her throat constrict—

Please, she whisper-thought, please—

———◄◆►———

Lake picked up a little speed, but couldn't move as fast as he wanted because of his eyes. They had been improving gradually, and he could see reasonably well in the light now, but he still couldn't make out detail where there was shadow.

As he approached the bend, he eased against the hill and crouched down to his hands, half running and half crawling.

Slipping out to the point of the bend, he dropped into low rocks. Around the bend there was a grove of cottonwood and a paddock of grass. The stream twisted back in the trees, cutting out a bank.

Squinting, Lake tried to pick out some kind of form or movement, but it was no good. Beyond a few feet the trees blurred, blending into themselves. Shadows and snow. Leaves rustling in the slight wind.

The scraping sound came again. Through the trees and down the bank. Squinting, Lake tried again to catch any form or motion, but it was still no good.

"Damn," he sighed and eased himself up, slipping through the rocks, across a small opening, then plunged into the trees.

Crouching down, he caught his breath. He could just make out the top of the bank now. Maybe twenty feet away. A blurred line in the trees. He still couldn't see any movement. Dropping down to his hands and knees, he began crawling.

Down the bank, he heard the sound again, and he crawled faster, pushing through the bushes and low limbs heavy with snow.

In front of him, the bank rose up slightly, then dropped. On the other side he heard the scraping again.

Lake hesitated. Sitting back on his feet, he swallowed and turned the knife edge up. Then pushing himself up, he climbed the bank quietly. Pressing to the top and over it.

Below him, he saw a riderless pony. There was a blanket and cinch on him and his reins trailed in the water of the stream as he fed on the new grass there. It was an Indian pony.

Lake's eyes jerked back over the bank. There was no one there. Turning, he peered back into the trees.

Where the hell was he? Lake wondered. He had to be somewhere close to—

Lake paused for a moment, then pressed back up against the bank and looked at the horse again.

His reins, he thought, and looked at them weaving in the stream. They weren't tied. The horse was loose.

Crawling on up on the bank cautiously, Lake looked at the horse, examining him. There were cuts on his back and legs. The blanket was torn nearly off, and the animal limped as he walked, favoring his right foreleg.

Lake stood up and, sheathing the knife, he glanced around, then brought his eyes back to the horse.

"A runaway," he said aloud to himself, then remembering Maggie, he called toward the bend.

"Mrs. Calder," he said. At the sound of his voice, the horse's head came up and he moved away into the pasture on the other side.

The answer was hesitant. "Mr. Mattick?"

"Yes," he replied. "It's all right. Come on down."

His eyes still on the horse, Lake descended the bank, and walked across the sandbar toward the water.

He was a few feet from the stream when he saw the dark scrawls in the snow and sand. He knelt down and was examining them when Maggie came around the bend, leading the three horses.

Standing, he held his hand out. "Stay there a minute," he called, his eyes moving over the ground.

"What is it?" she called.

"Hoof tracks," he answered. "Unshod and a lot of them." He made his way back down to her slowly.

"Unshod?"

"Indian ponies," Lake answered and pointed to the animal grazing in the pasture. "Like that one."

"There's another one," Maggie said. "Way at the other end of the meadow."

Lake nodded. "Figures."

"Is that what we heard?"

"Yes."

"Where are their riders?"

Lake crouched back down, looking at the tracks again.

"Mr. Mattick?"

He stood up looking off northeast. "The bluff would be that way," he said to himself. "And Rufe said this is the nearest water this side of the bluff.

"What—?"

Lake turned. "The bluff," he said, "is that way."

"What has that got to do with the horses having no riders?"

"That's what I'm getting at," Lake explained walking to her. "There are a lot of tracks around here. Four or five horses, and the one I saw was marked up pretty badly. Hurt." He looked back in the direction of the bluff. "We lost horses and men back there, and I think they did too. That's why we haven't seen them. They were tryin' to catch up their animals. I'd say about half of them are on foot. That leaves four or five on horseback. With a couple running holding on to the horses' tails, there are maybe seven still after us." He looked at the loose horses. "And those animals came this way because they were thirsty and this is the only water—"

Maggie blinked. "Mr. Kitrel," she said and turned toward her horse. Reaching out, Lake grasped her arm.

"Where you goin'?"

"To Mr. Kitrel. If there are only that many, we—"

Lake was shaking his head. "That's the hell of it. It doesn't do us any good."

"We can fight them—"

"We're nearly out of ammunition."

"Mr. Kitrel has a rifle—"

Lake nodded. "That's right. But it still doesn't make any difference. We've got three in the Henry. In a close fight, Rufe could get off two or three shots. Maybe, by some miracle, four." He shook his head. "We'd have to make ever' shot count, and nobody's that good, Mrs. Calder. Nobody. Besides"—he frowned—"we're not sure of any of this. It's all guesswork."

Maggie stared at him. "You're going to leave him—"

"We already have."

"But he's got a chance now," she protested.

"Dammit, Mrs. Calder, can't you understand? He doesn't. Likely none of us do."

She shook her head unbelievingly. "You don't care about anything or anybody, do you? Just survival and being right." She turned toward the horses.

"Mrs. Calder—"

"I owe him," she said, and kept walking, then added, "So do you. He got himself wounded helping you." Gathering up the reins to the blue, she mounted her horse, then looked down at the rifle in her hand.

"Mr. Kitrel will need this," she said. "Do you mind if I keep it?"

Lake shook his head. "No, I don't mind."

"Besides"—she pointed to his horse—"you've still got your damned saber. You can use that on Quincy," she said and, pulling her horse's head around, she strapped him out, running back the way they'd come.

Lake watched her round the bend, then shaking his head, he walked to the Morgan. Grasping the saddle, he leaned against the leather and closed his eyes.

"No way," he growled. Going back would be stupid. It didn't make sense.

"No sense at all," he said aloud and, opening his eyes, he mounted the Morgan and turned him downstairs.

Across the creek, the Indian ponies were still grazing in the meadow. Lake eased back on the Morgan's reins and hesitated, watching them.

It was too much of a gamble, he told himself. Nothing had changed. Not really. It was— Lake frowned, and leaned forward on the pommel of the saddle.

"Damn," he sighed. It was no use. He had to try. Because Maggie was right. He owed Rufe. And not just for the arrow he'd taken.

Pulling the Morgan around, he spurred him back up the stream. Running, it didn't take him long to catch up with Maggie.

She looked up at the sound of his horse's hooves and watched him come in beside her.

They rode a few feet, then wordlessly, she handed him his rifle and he slipped it in its boot.

CHAPTER 21

Rufe Kitrel waited. He had gone through the ritual of checking the Hawken, then loading it. The stiffness from his shoulder slowed him, but he didn't care. He enjoyed the process. It gave him something to do.

When he was finished with the Hawken, he slipped his Green River from its scabbard and sharpened it on the rock next to him, then placed it on the rock along with his powder horn, a patch and ball, and percussion cap.

Now, he waited. His eyes concentrating on the far ridge. He would have about twenty minutes from the time they came over it until they came out of the trees. Using his knee as a support, he would be able to aim and drop one there.

Then as they were charging him, he would try to re-load. With the fixin's laid out next to him and ready, he thought he could do it, even with his bad shoulder. He would have maybe a minute, and that should give him plenty of time. He just wouldn't have time to aim. But that didn't matter. By then, they would be right on top of him, and he wouldn't need to.

He nodded. He would likely be able to take two with him. Three, if he was lucky and could get to his Green River.

A thin smile tugged his lips. If he was lucky. Hell, if he was lucky, he ought to toss'em for it.

The smile pushed into a laugh. Likely a bad idea any-how, he mused. Likely none of'em would have a coin.

He shook his head. Gettin' addled, he concluded. "Old," he sighed, and the laugh ebbed away. Now don't go feelin' sorry for yourself, he thought and looked up.

Above him, the sky was clear and the mist had begun to drift away from the peaks. A calm breathed through him. Like a part of the mists and peaks. He just wished that Dick—

A flicker on the top of the far ridge jerked his eyes around, and his hand tightened on the Hawken. It was just a blur of movement and color at first. Then a man.

Lake and Maggie rode hard. Rounding a small hill, they pushed back up into the pine and spruce at the bottom of the valley and angled toward the high ridge where they had left Rufe.

As they came up over a small rise in the trees, Lake reined in and squinted through the shifting trunks, his eyes following the line of the ridge. It took him a few minutes, but he finally spotted the old man. Partially hidden in the rocks. But still there.

He smiled and was turning to Maggie, when she gripped his arm, hard, pointing up through the trees toward the valley. Lake followed her gesture and saw them —the Absorakas—coming down the low ridge.

"Get down," he whispered to Maggie, and they dismounted hurriedly, then pushed the horses back down behind the drop of the hill.

Climbing back to the top of the slope, Lake knelt down, then laid out flat, watching the Indians. Maggie tied the horses to a low branch, then crawled up beside him.

The Indians were strung out in a dark line. Pushing down the ridge, starting into the valley.

Seven, Lake counted. At first he thought there were more, then realized that two of the men with horses were on the ground, leading their animals. Resting them. Three were riding, and the last two brought up the rear, holding on to the tails of the horses. Seven men, five horses.

A hard way to travel. Lake nodded.

Lake looked from the Indians to Rufe. "He'll hit when they come out of the trees," Lake thought aloud. "We've got maybe ten minutes until then."

Maggie's eyes fell, and she shook her head. "You were right," she whispered.

Lake looked at her. "What—?"

"There's nothing we can do. There probably never was."

Lake swallowed, fear clouding his eyes. A hopeless ache stretched through him, and he could feel himself trembling, the edge of panic pressing at him with the memory of Dick Summers. He had thought he would die, and he did. He had gone through a war and let a friend die because he had thought there was nothing he could do. Because he had thought . . .

"Nothing . . ." Maggie whispered again.

And he looked up. "Yes, there is," he replied.

"What?"

Blinking, he stared at her, realizing he didn't have an answer. "Something." He nodded, his gaze moving back to the Indians. Then Rufe. "We can catch them in a cross fire." He started figuring, then tightened his fist against his leg in frustration. "Dammit," he growled. "If I just had two or three more shells . . ." He shook his head. "I'd better get to it," he said and slipped down to the horses, jerked his Henry from its boot, then turned to Maggie.

"I've got to leave you," he said with difficulty, and pulled his knife from its sheath, and handed it to her. "Wish I had a better weapon for you."

Taking the knife, she nodded. "I understand."

She smiled wanly. "I . . . wouldn't know what to do with it. . . ."

"Yeah." Lake frowned. "Saber's not good for much. Just at ceremonies and in a charge." He glanced back over the crest of the hill. "Guess I better—" he began, and his voice stopped suddenly.

Then hesitating, he turned, looking back down at the saber on the Morgan. Staring at it.

"Jesus," he whispered. "That's crazy."

Maggie's eyes narrowed. "What?"

Lake didn't answer her. Instead, he looked to the Indians, then the slope in front of Rufe between the old man and the tree line and let his eyes follow the ridge line down to where it ended, blending into the ground below them. He was silent a moment, then swung his gaze back to the Indians.

"The horses—" He nodded.

"Mr. Mattick," Maggie insisted. "Will you—?"

Lake turned to her. Taking the knife from her hand, he slipped it into her coat pocket. "Keep that," he said, cutting her off. "You may still need it."

Before she could say anything, he shoved the rifle into her hands. "You know how to use this?" he asked.

She nodded. "I think so, but—"

"Just lever and fire. Don't try to hit anything. Aim at their horses' feet," he said, pushing away and down to the Morgan.

Maggie followed him and watched with a mixture of amazement and confusion as he mounted his horse.

"Fire right after Rufe does," he went on. "When you empty the Henry, ride for Rufe. Get him mounted, then get out of here."

"All right," she said. "But what?"

"Fighting them is one way of doing this, Mrs. Calder," he answered quickly. "Scattering their horses is another."

"Scattering their—" Maggie stammered. "How?"

"The only way we've got left," he said, wheeling the Morgan. "I'm going to charge."

CHAPTER 22

Lake pushed the Morgan to the bottom of the hill, then following the ridge down he crossed it where it blended back into the ground.

On the backside of the ridge, Lake reined in for a moment and stood in the saddle, trying to spot the old man.

The ex-soldier hadn't completely figured what he was going to do yet. But if he could reach Rufe before he fired, maybe they could co-ordinate something. Frowning, Lake shook his head.

He couldn't see Rufe. You picked a good spot, old man,

Lake thought, sinking back into the saddle, then strapped the horse out, angling toward where he thought Rufe should be.

The Morgan pulled hard up the slope, and Lake prayed that he hadn't cut it too thin. The crest seemed to be a long way away, coming toward him only by inches.

He strapped the Morgan and he could feel the big horse respond, stretching, reaching for more ground. They came up to within a few yards of the crest, and Lake hauled the animal in again, trying to pick Rufe out of the rocks. Still nothing. He must have figured short.

"Dammit," he growled.

Rufe had to be along here someplace. Maybe— The crack of a shot jerked the ex-soldier's eyes up. It was Rufe's Hawken. Not far down the ridge. He hadn't missed him by much.

But it didn't matter now. Rufe had started the ball rolling.

Turning up the slope, Lake spurred the Morgan, then reached back, his hand closing around the handle of the saber, slipping it free of its scabbard, sliding the blade into the cold light. Whispering as if there were memory there.

Running, he heard the second shot. Maggie, he nodded, and bursting over the crest of the ridge, he plunged down the other side.

Out of the corner of his eye, he could half see Rufe in the rocks.

"Stay down," he yelled at the old man, then strapping the Morgan, he concentrated on the Indians. Placing them. They were sixty or seventy yards down, just above the tree line, a whorl of confusion.

One man was down, sprawled in the snow. Above him a small gray horse was loose, rearing. Rufe had taken one of the riders. Two were still on horseback. A man on a black. The other on an appaloosa. Both near the tree line. The man on the black had lost one rein, and his horse was swinging back down the hill.

The appaloosa crowhopped, kicking frantically at the other horses and the two riders on the ground, who were between Lake and the men on horseback, trying to get back aboard their mounts. But it was no good. The shots had spooked them, and the men trying to control them panicked them even more.

The Henry crashed again, and the dead man's gray backpedaled, reeling down the hill, and one of the men without a horse lunged for the animal, grasping for the reins, and as he did, Lake caught a glimpse of his face. It was the dead boy's father. He had run all that way. Rearing, the gray tore loose and plunged into the trees, and the dead boy's father went after him.

The other man on foot was running for cover. Ducking into the trees—

———◄◆►———

Levering the Henry, Maggie brought the rifle back up, when she saw the Indian coming at her. At first she couldn't believe it.

Lowering the rifle, she blinked. He was still coming. Like a memory she had remembered before it happened.

The Indian jumped a downed log and was twisting through the trees. Running a jagged course. Ramming through snow-laden branches. Fifty feet away.

Her first reaction was to run, but she found she couldn't move. Her eyes were fixed on the charging man. She could see his face now and hear his breathing mixing with the sound of his running.

Forcing herself, she raised the rifle. Leveling it on him. Placing the barrel on the broadest part of his chest. The Indian weaved, and Maggie held her fire.

Twenty feet. He whooped at her, but she held the rifle steady. Waiting.

Ten feet. Inside, she felt herself screaming—widening through her like a chasm into oblivion, but she held her fire.

He weaved again. Then charged straight at her, coming until she could see nothing but him.

And she fired.

The slug hit him just below the neck, spinning him back around in a half tumble, slamming him down into the snow. He tried to move. To get up. Then he slumped back into the soft whiteness. And was quiet.

Staring at him, Maggie kept the rifle trained on him. Somewhere, she heard somebody sobbing, and realized that it was her. For a moment, the trees and snow and dead man seemed to wash around her, surrounding and filling her, and she thought she was going to throw up or faint.

Movement on the slope tugged her eyes up and around. Mechanically, she levered the rifle, swinging it back up the slope and pulling the trigger. The hammer fell on an empty chamber.

Maggie lowered the rifle, staring at it, then turning, she pushed down the hill to the horses.

On the ridge, Rufe wondered for a moment what the hell was going on. First, when he had seen the Absoraka, he thought the Indians had split up. Then there were the shots and Mattick—

He shook his head. It didn't matter. He would find out the way later. If he lived that long. Stiffly, he began reloading.

Below him, Mattick had already closed the gap between him and the bunched-up Absorakas, taking the lead Indian on the ground first.

The warrior stood his ground. Caught in the confusion, he had lost his horse. Distracted by Maggie's shots and his rearing horse, he had not seen Lake coming down on him, until the last moment. He turned to face the charging horseman, trying to get an arrow out of his sheath. But he had lost too much time.

Lake angled the Morgan straight into the Indian, knocking him off his feet. Reeling his horse out to one side, Lake swung his saber across the man's hip as the Indian tried to regain his feet, sending him sprawling and bleeding into the snow.

Now Lake was turning on the second man who had been running, leading his horse. Lake drove the Morgan into the Indian as he was lunging at his horse, grasping the animal's mane, trying to get back aboard.

The Morgan's chest caught the Indian full in the back, ramming him into his horse. The Indian sank like a drowning man. Recovering from the shock of the impact, Lake forced his mount over the fallen body and into the Indian's rearing horse, pushing it back into the two mounted men.

The man on the black caught most of it. He had just caught up his loose rein when Lake's horse plunged into him. His black reared, and fighting to stay on him, the brave swung his horse down the hill.

The man on the appaloosa recovered quickly, wheeled in the opposite direction. Straight into Lake.

Lake rushed alongside the Indian as he was turning. Bringing the tip of the blade up, he thrust it through the man on the appaloosa.

The force of the blow doubled the brave, knocking him backward. Falling, he twisted, reaching vainly for Lake as he died.

Still capitalizing on the element of surprise, Lake wheeled his horse to pursue the man on the black, who was now racing for safety in the pines.

———————————◄◆►———————————

Finishing loading, Rufe raised his Hawken jerkily and tried to follow the fleeing man on the black, but it was no use. It was too quick a shot. He'd been able to take the man on the gray because he had had time. Now he didn't. Besides, he might hit Lake.

Lowering the Hawken, he frowned, then saw the running figure of the Indian trying to catch up the loose gray in the pines.

He dragged the Hawken up again, following the moving target through the kaleidoscope of trees. The Indian was in the open for a brief second and Rufe fired. The ball blew a hunk out of a tree trunk, and the Indian kept running.

"Dammit," Rufe growled and started to reload again, when he saw something else move in the trees. It was Maggie. Pushing her horse hard. Leading the blue. Coming for him.

———◆——

Down the ridge, Lake tore the Morgan around, spurring him hard, clattering across the slope, into the trees after the man on the black.

Lake was closing on him when the Indian pulled his pony around and downhill, into the pines, weaving the black horse between the trunks, leading Lake deep into the trees. Then, in a surprise move, the brave turned back on his pursuer, a tomahawk in his hand.

As the Indian came around the trunk of a shielding pine he swung at Lake. Lake spurred the Morgan forward and deflected the tomahawk with the blade of the saber. As the two horses lunged into each other, Morgan slipped his foot free of its stirrup and kicked the Indian in the stomach.

The man on the black reeled, and as he did, Lake used the momentum to shove the tomahawk back and away.

He then swung the handguard of the saber around, ramming it into the Indian's face, hitting him with a solid blow, knocking him backward into the snow.

The black pony reared, backing away from Lake and his fallen, unconscious rider. Lake waved the saber and shouted, sending the animal running through the trees. Standing in the saddle, he looked for the other horses. They were all loose and running. Except one.

Down the slope beyond the trees, the dead boy's father had caught up the gray and was swinging up on him.

"Dammit," Lake growled, and turning, looked to the top of the ridge. Maggie had gotten the old man on his horse, and they were headed down the ridge.

Lake's eyes went back to the remaining Indian. What was it Rufe had said about him? That he would follow them into hell. . . . And he would, Lake agreed. He knew he would.

For an instant, staring at the Indian, Lake knew that man better than he had ever known anyone.

"Yeah," Lake whispered and spurred the Morgan out. In the valley, the Indian unsheathed his knife and rode to meet him.

Hammering down the slope and through the trees, the snowspray from the Morgan's hooves blurred around him, but the man coming at him was always clear. A reflection in dark webbed glass.

Falling, Lake managed to get hold of the Indian's knife hand at the wrist, and gripping it hard, he dragged the Indian with him as he tumbled back out of the saddle and crashed to the ground.

The two men rolled in the snow and came to a halt

with Lake on the bottom. He tried to lift the saber up, but the blade was buried in the snow and the weight of the snow slowed the blade enough to let the brave clutch Lake's wrist and push the saber back down.

Wrestling, Lake could smell the man now. Smell him and feel his breath against his. Straining. Trembling.

Above him, Lake felt the brave bringing his knee forward, scraping through the snow. Then lifting Lake's saber hand, the Indian slipped his knee under Lake's arm and pushed. Leaning into it with all his weight.

He's breaking it, Lake thought, and releasing the saber, he was able to shove the arm up between them, snapping the Indian's hold. Ramming the hand on through, Lake pounded it into the Indian's shoulder and twisted the knife hand.

The Indian pushed himself up and flung himself over on his back, tumbling down the slope. Lake held on, rolling with him, hurdling over the Indian, then down into the snow again.

Using the momentum, the ex-soldier turned, getting his feet under him, jacking himself into a standing position, and backhanded the Indian in the face with his free arm.

The Indian staggered back and Lake swung his free arm up under the brave's arm he held, wrenching it at the same time, bending it until he thought it would break. But it didn't.

The Indian stumbled backward, and Lake hit him in the chest, shoving him down, then swung his fist up, battering the Indian's arm again.

It didn't break, but Lake felt the hold on the knife loosen, then give. The knife dropped into the snow.

Letting go of the arm, Lake shoved the Indian away and wheeled, looking for the knife, but the Indian was too quick for him. He caught Lake in the lower back, punching the wind from him, pounding him into the ground.

Cawing for air, his mouth full of snow, Lake fought the darkness thickening behind his eyes, and turned back into the Indian, pushing a nightmare weak fist into his side. Amazingly, the Indian fell off him, slumping into the snow.

Lake dragged himself over on his back, and for a moment the two tiring men lay in the snow staring at each other, their breaths raking through them making a raw sound.

Then, suddenly, the Indian was up on his hands and knees, crawling, coming at Lake. Lake shoved himself up, diving at the Indian, slamming his elbow into the other man's mouth, ramming him backward, and they both tumbled down the slope, plowing through the snow.

Sliding to a stop, Lake pulled his eyes up and could see the Indian staggering to his feet. Lake rose to meet him.

The two men fell into each other, weary arms trying for a hold and not succeeding. Lake was weakening fast and he knew it. Pushing away from the Indian, Lake hit the brave a glancing blow in the stomach, then backhanded him in the face.

The Indian stumbled, then marched back into Lake, closing his hands around the white man's throat. Lake hit him in the stomach, but it did no good. The hands were fast.

Pivoting, Lake lifted his boot and stomped it down into

the Indian's moccasined foot. For the first time, Lake heard a sound from the Indian. A slight bark, but no more. And the hands on his neck weakened. Lake hit him again in the stomach, then in the face.

The hands opened and Lake had to think about it to get the strength to bring his fist up, hammering it through the Indian's jaw, knocking him back down the slope, stumbling into a fallen log. The Indian's feet came out from under him and he crashed over the log and back into the snow.

Struggling, he tried to get up, but Lake rushed into him kicking him in the face. The Indian slumped back, one foot on the log, his breath pumping his chest.

Lake wheeled looking back up the slope, his eyes scanning it until he saw the handle of his saber jutting out of the white.

Slogging back up the slope, he reached down and drew the weapon from the whiteness. He was turning to the Morgan a few feet away when he saw movement through the trees. The men he'd ridden down were getting up. In the pines, the man who had been on the black was rousing too. Frowning, Lake caught up the Morgan quickly and walked back down the incline.

The dead boy's father was still sprawled in the snow, and his eyes fluttered open as Lake came down to him, then stood above him, the saber in his hand. The Indian pushed his hands under him, trying to get up, then fell back, his breath coming hard.

Swallowing, he raised his eyes to meet Lake's. There was no fear in them. Lake's hand tightened on the saber handle, and he raised the blade.

Pausing, he stared down at the man and lowered the saber, then in one quick move, he brought his foot up and rammed it down into the leg resting on the log. The bone snapped like a branch breaking, and the Indian screamed, twisting into the snow.

Lake turned back up the hill and mounted the Morgan hurriedly. The other Absorakas were on their feet now, staggering toward them.

Lake kicked the Morgan out, riding down the valley, catching up the gray and shouting him out. At the bottom of the valley, he came in beside Rufe and Maggie, then reined up. Slipping the saber back in its scabbard, he looked back. The others had reached the boy's father.

Next to him, the old man shook his head. "Not that I'm complainin' you understand, but I am a tad curious. How come you to come back?"

Lake glanced at him. "I found a horse," he said.

"A what?" Rufe asked.

"I'll tell you later," Lake said, his eyes drifting back to the Indians again. Rufe followed his gaze.

"Why didn't you kill him?" the old man finally asked.

Lake eased back around front in the saddle and shrugged. "I couldn't," he answered. "I knew how he felt. . . ." His voice trailed and he shook his head. "Hell, I don't know, Rufe. I just didn't."

The old man smiled tightly and nodded. "Well, it don't matter now. It's over."

"No," Lake said, nudging the Morgan out. "Not yet. Not till we get to Cunningham's."

CHAPTER 23

Cunningham's came into sight a little after noon the next day.

They had ridden all night, stopping only once at the creek where Lake and Maggie had spotted the Indian horses. They watered their own animals and Maggie attended to Rufe's shoulder. She offered to look at the graze on Lake's chest, but he just shook his head, mounting up, saying he didn't have the time.

As they rode into the stockade, Lake was able to make out four wagon encampments around it. His eyes moved continually, then at the gates of the stockade, he reined the Morgan in and frowned.

"Too many." He shook his head and looked to Rufe. "Where would they know?" he asked.

"Bar, I reckon," the old man answered and, nudging his horse out, he angled toward the large main building that dominated the inside of the stockade. Signs above the porch designated the sections of the building. Store, hotel, and saloon.

Rufe pulled up in front of the saloon and dismounted stiffly.

Lake and Maggie followed him down, and Lake took the saber and Henry off his horse.

Maggie turned to Rufe. "Shouldn't you see somebody about that shoulder?"

"Cotton—the bartender—does most of the doctorin' 'round here. 'Sides, you fixed it pretty good back there at the creek. Come on, I'll buy you a cup of coffee—that is unless you want to go on to the hotel and check on the coach—"

"No"—Maggie shook her head—"it can wait."

"Ain't changed your mind have you?"

"No," she answered, watching Lake mount the steps. "I'm still going. The coffee sounds good."

Rufe glanced at Lake. "Yeah." He nodded.

Lake crossed the porch and pushed through the double doors into the bar.

It was a lot like the one at Calder's. A long, narrow room. Dark. A slab of rough-cut pine, smooth side up on two huge stumps across from the door. A few tables scattered in the dim light.

The room was empty except for the bartender, sitting on a stool, leaning on the bar, half-asleep. He was a big man, well over six feet, with bear-greased hair and arms almost as thick as the stumps supporting the bar. Lake crossed to the bar and Maggie and Rufe came in.

"Hello, Cotton," Rufe said, leaning up against the slab.

The bartender's head bobbed up and he blinked. "Who's that?"

"Rufe Kitrel."

The bartender rubbed his face and stepped down from the stool.

"Old Rufe," he yawned. "How you doin'?"

"Fair. How 'bout some coffee and the stuff you use to strangle snakes?"

"Comin' up." The bartender nodded, then squinting, he saw Rufe's shoulder. "What the hell you done to yourself, hoss?"

"Got crossways with some Absorakas."

Cotton pointed to a chair. "Sit down and I'll—"

"In a bit." Rufe nodded. "First I want to get some deadener in me."

"Yeah," Cotton agreed. "That's best." He looked to Lake and Maggie. "You folks?"

"Same," Lake answered.

"I'll just have the coffee," Maggie said.

"And do one for yourself," Rufe added. "Don't want you workin' on me sober."

Cotton placed three glasses on the slab and poured. Rufe, Lake, and Cotton downed the whiskey.

"Speakin' of snakes—" the old man wheezed, setting the glass back on the bar.

"Yeah?" Cotton coughed.

"How many were in that barrel?"

"Not more'n a couple. Don't want to foul it. Get that coffee now," he said and, leaving the bottle, he turned toward the stove at the other end of the room.

Lake poured himself another drink. Maggie watched the bartender walk away, then looked at Lake.

"Mr. Mattick—" she began.

"Not now," he snapped, cutting her off, then frowned. "Not now," he repeated, softening his voice.

The bartender brought the coffee and Lake looked up at him.

"A week and a half ago—" he began.

Cotton nodded. "Yeah?"

"There was a train, run by—"

"They're all still here," Cotton nodded. "Storm kept any of'em from leavin'. Waitin' yet to see that the weather holds. If you're tryin' to catch up with one of'em, you're in luck."

"Yeah." Lake frowned, nodding. Reaching out, he grasped the saber, hard, then sighing, shook his head. "Hell," he sighed, and raised his eyes to the bartender. "Do me a favor will you—?"

"If I can." Cotton shrugged.

"There's a man named Quincy with one of the trains. Tell him Lake Mattick was through."

"Quincy." The bartender's eyes narrowed. "Name sounds familiar."

"He's probably a good customer. Just tell him, will you?"

"Sure. But why don't you—?"

"I . . . I'm in a hurry," Lake said and turned toward Rufe. "You said somethin' about headin' back up in those mountains. I got my musterin' out pay if you're still game."

The old man grinned. "You're mighty well told I am. What about your schoolteachin'?"

"Someday, maybe." Lake shrugged. "Why don't you let Cotton take care of that shoulder and we'll—"

"And your chest and eyes," Maggie put in.

"They're fine," Lake said, then smiled, seeing the protest beginning in Maggie's eyes. "All right"—he nodded—"then I'm—"

Suddenly Cotton looked up. "Say, Mattick—"

"Yeah?"

"You say that fella's name was Quincy?"

Lake nodded. "Yeah."

"He ex-army?"

"A major."

The bartender slapped the plank nodding. "Knew I knew him."

"Like I said—"

"Ain't nobody gonna tell him nothin'," the bartender interrupted. "He's dead."

Lake turned staring at him. "What?"

The bartender nodded. "Didn't recollect him, by that name. Always wanted to be called Major. Got himself all likkered up in here two days ago and wandered out in that storm. Found him yesterday stiffer'n a board and deader'n hell. Drank in here all the time. Never could hold it."

"No," Lake said, "he never could."

28

Turning, he walked out on the porch and stood for a moment, then looked up as Rufe and Maggie followed him out.

"What I can't figure out," Lake sighed, "is why I feel sorry for him." He shook his head slowly. "Damn . . ." He was quiet for a moment, then suddenly an odd bark burst from his lips. He was laughing and crying at the same time, and slowly he sat down on the steps, the laughter coming harder now.

Maggie and Rufe stared at him, then they were laughing too, and sitting down they joined him on the step.

The bartender came to the door, frowning. "Listen here," he snapped. "Don't care how he died. A fella's passin' ain't funny. . . ."

Rufe turned and looked at him. "Don't you see," he sighed. "Funny ain't got nothin' to do with it?"

Blinking, the bartender stared at the three of them sitting there, laughing harder now, tears streaming down their faces, and he remembered that sound from a long time ago. The sound of the boys at the rendezvous.

"*Companyeros,*" he whispered, and drawn by the sound of the laughter, he sat down with them.